"I'm on fire, Red.

Cash dropped into the b
beside Larinda and pull
"Let's finish last night. Now."

"Here?" She had never made love in a car, didn't know the first thing about it. Cash seemed to know, though. He pushed the front seats to a forward slant and eased her down beneath him.

"Pretend we're two teenagers at a drive-in movie," he murmured, filling his hands with her hair.

She traced her trembling fingers over his lips. "I wasn't that kind of girl."

"Well, I was that kind of boy. I still am."

"I feel like a very bad girl here with you."

"You don't look like one." He slid her sweater up and off. "You look too beautiful to be bad...."

Seeing Red

ROSEANNE WILLIAMS

MILLS & BOON LIMITED
ETON HOUSE, 18-24 PARADISE ROAD
RICHMOND, SURREY TW9 1SR

*First published in Great Britain in 1994
by Mills & Boon Limited, Eton House, 18-24 Paradise Road,
Richmond, Surrey TW9 1SR*

© Sheila Slattery 1993

ISBN 0 263 78788 5

21 - 9407

*Printed in Great Britain by
BPC Paperbacks Ltd
A member of
The British Printing Company Ltd*

1

LARINDA OUTLAW WAS stone broke the day she inherited a drive-in movie theater from a man she didn't know.

She only knew *of* Jethro Everly. He had been her godfather. Beyond showing up for her christening, however, he had not performed one godfatherly act from that day forward. No visits, no phone calls, no birthday cards, nothing.

So Larinda was astonished when she received a letter from his attorney on her twenty-eighth birthday advising that Mr. Everly had died without surviving family and that he had named her in his will. The drive-in theater had been a long-running investment, the letter said, the only one Jethro hadn't sold to pay debts. He had managed it from a distance for years. Now it was hers.

Hers! Four months after a hurricane had decimated the video store she'd owned and operated in Texas, something of value was hers again. Something that would earn her a living again.

Thank God. She'd been forced to take refuge at her parents' house in her hometown of Anaheim, California, since the disaster. Now she suddenly had the prospect of a fresh start. Hopeful for the first time since the hurricane —and thinking kind thoughts of her godfather for the first time ever—Larinda drove thirty miles from Anaheim to Hollywood to meet with the attorney. She found his office in a building that had seen finer days during the silent-movie era.

The appearance of both the building and the attorney dimmed her initial bright hopes. He was a Danny De Vito look-alike, complete with ponytail and aloha shirt. His name was even Vito. Morey Vito.

The tropical motif extended beyond his shirt to his office decor. *Only in Hollywood*, Larinda thought. As she walked to his desk, Morey blatantly ogled her long, fiery red hair. The only reputable sign she could see was his Harvard law degree on the wall.

"The drive-in is apparently somewhat run-down," Morey told her after she'd settled into one of the peacock chairs facing his desk. "Selling it 'as is' would be one way to go if you happen to need cash."

Larinda almost leaped out of the chair with renewed hope at that last word. After losing her sole source of income in the hurricane, she needed cash in the worst way. Her insurance company still hadn't paid off on her loss of Outlaw Home Video.

"However," he continued, "the terms of the will forbid any sale, or negotiation to sell, until Chester Bowman's lease runs out in twelve months."

"Whose lease?" Larinda frowned. "For what?"

"For the flea market Bowman operates on the property," Morey elaborated, lighting a cigar before asking, "You don't mind if I smoke, do you?"

If Larinda hadn't been a big Danny De Vito fan, she'd have minded. One of his biggest, she let it pass and inquired, "Why is there a flea market on the property?"

"It's one way drive-in theater owners stay in the black these days," he explained between puffs of blue smoke. "They run flea markets on the property during the day and show movies after dark. However, Jethro stopped showing movies years ago after he made the final mortgage payment."

She looked at Morey with intense brown eyes. "Stopped? Why?"

"The profit margin narrowed over the years, plus he hired bad managers. It's been just a flea market since then, earning Bowman a modest living. For you, the lease income will cover overhead and property taxes, but won't earn you a living unless you show movies and pack the viewers in. That's a decision you'll have to—" Morey's phone buzzed, cutting him off. "I'll just be a second."

The second stretched into minutes as Morey dickered with a rival attorney on the other end of the line. Larinda used the first few moments to mentally curse Chester Bowman's lease. She needed cash *now*, not a year from now. Might there be a way around this stumbling block? She crossed her fingers that there was.

The next few minutes she spent puzzling over why Jethro had bequeathed her the drive-in. Guilt was the most obvious answer, but she was all too aware that afflictions of conscience were non-existent in Jethro's profession. She'd learned that from her parents' experience with him. He had been their Hollywood agent in their early days as movie hopefuls. Promising to make them superstars, he had changed their last name from Smith to Outlaw, gotten them bit parts in *Wild West*, then dropped them as soon as he found better prospects.

For Larinda, that was proof enough of Jethro's lack of conscience. However, she reminded herself, *Wild West* had been enough to leave Larry and Linda Outlaw forever grateful to Jethro. It had become a Western film classic as well as their only claim to being actors.

That was why they had asked Jethro to be the sole god-parent of the first child.

But she couldn't see why Jethro had agreed; he'd had a dozen Hollywood superstars under contract by that time. In contrast, her parents were already has-beens, with many lean years ahead of them. This was before they'd begun working in the delicatessen they later bought. Jethro could have declined being her godfather, but he hadn't.

Guilt must have finally caught up with him, just as her parents had finally become financially responsible.

"That's show biz, kid," Linda and Larry had said after she'd grown old enough to ask why her godfather never phoned, wrote or visited.

She now wondered how much Jethro's attorney had known about him. According to Larry and Linda, Jethro had been a high roller in his day. He'd never gone anywhere without a starlet on his arm and a star-maker contract in his vest pocket. They'd both seen him conduct four separate phone conversations all at one time. Their favorite quirky anecdote about him was that he'd always refused to eat any food that was red.

"Two more seconds," Morey whispered, covering the mouthpiece with his palm. "I swear."

Larinda continued to puzzle over her godfather. She recalled how, after graduating from high school, she had read in a gossip column that his once-stellar cast of stars had steadily diminished over the years. "*That's* show biz," she had told her parents with teenage satisfaction.

She had given no thought to Jethro in the years that followed. After high school had come two years of college for her and then a job offer from a friend in Texas to manage a video store. As an avid movie lover, she'd readily accepted. When her friend's divorce required the sacrifice sale of the store, Larinda had bought it and made a good business out of it for five years.

Just as she had achieved the financial security she had craved after a childhood spent in financial straits, the hurricane had ripped away everything she had worked so hard to attain.

Now, having come home to work in the deli and wait for her insurance claim to be paid off, she was being told she would have to wait again. Twelve months before she could sell her inherited property? All because of a stipulation in Jethro's will regarding the flea-market lease? There had to be a way to regain what she had lost. She tapped her toe, thinking.

"Sorry about that," the attorney said, hanging up at last. "As I was saying—" He looked blank for a moment. "What was I saying?"

"I think it was something about Jethro," Larinda replied. "Did you know him well?"

Morey blew a smoke ring. "Never met him until he decided he needed a will a few months before he died. I've heard around town that he was a real eccentric. Wouldn't eat anything that was red, if you can believe that."

So much for determining why an eccentric had left a drive-in theater to a neglected godchild. "Would you know if Chester Bowman might be agreeable to negotiating the lease?" she asked.

Morey's shrug was noncommittal. "I believe Jethro knew Bowman from way back, so he must be near retirement. Would he like to retire? Good question. He hasn't responded to my letters. I've phoned several times, but no answer."

"Is he aware that the property has been willed to me?"

"He's been notified by registered mail."

"Well, that's a start," she said, coming to a quick, firm decision. "I'll just pay him a visit and try to negotiate with him."

"No harm in trying," Morey said. Then he added, "If Bowman won't budge, you can always show movies until the lease runs out."

"Right," she said, not particularly interested in that option. Ten minutes later, she had signed the papers that gave her title to The Moonglow Drive-in Theater.

ARMED WITH A ROAD MAP, she drove off the next morning in her father's aging Volkswagen van to inspect her drive-in. It was located two hundred miles northeast of Los Angeles in the San Joaquin Valley town of Weston. Larinda had never been there, but her mind was made up. She'd buy out Bowman's lease, with some of her insurance money—as soon as it came through—and sell the Moonglow.

There was no stipulation in the will against buying out the lease, after all. The will prevented her only from selling or negotiating a sale before Bowman's lease expired. If the lease became hers instead of Bowman's, she could sell.

Added to the insurance money due any day now, that would put her back in business with her own video store anywhere she liked in California. Here, where she had decided to stay near her parents and younger brother, there were no hurricanes to flatten and drown out five years of hard work.

Four months ago, living near family hadn't been as important to her as it was now. After surviving a natural disaster, she had a new appreciation for the ties that bind. Without her family, where would she have gone, homeless and unemployed? During the hurricane, she had prayed that she'd live to see her parents and her younger brother again. From the moment her prayer had been answered, she'd been determined to stick close to home.

After selling the Moonglow she'd settle somewhere. After selling, she'd also be in the money again. Only one thing stood in her way.

"Not for long, Chester old chum," she vowed, her eyes steady on the road, her grip firm on the steering wheel.

"DAD! Dad!"

At his son's call, Cash stepped back from refereeing an argument between two vendors at the Moonglow Flea Market. Driving the fingers of both hands through his wavy dark hair, he fixed seven-year-old Daniel with an exasperated gray gaze.

"What *is* it, Dan? Make it quick."

"Can I show Jeffie the movie projector, Dad? Pleeeze?"

No! Cash almost snapped at him before he caught himself and reached out to rumple the boy's wild blond curls. It wasn't Dan's fault that two crotchety rug sellers couldn't stand the sight of each other. "Promise you'll both just look and not touch?" he said, instead.

Dan stood at attention and held up his grubby right hand in a two-fingered salute. "Cub Scout's honor, Dad."

"Here you go, Scout." Cash pulled a key ring from the pocket of the forest green corduroys he wore and extracted the projection-room key. "Have it back to me in ten minutes on the nose."

"Yes, sir! Mucho thanks."

With a fond eye, Cash watched Daniel sprint off in search of Jeffie. Then he rolled the sleeves of his plaid flannel shirt to his elbows and squinted up at the sun. Though it was barely noon on Saturday, the fourth of March, it felt like the Fourth of July.

It was hot, getting hotter, and the feud between the Purvis brothers, Otis and Otto, was also heating up. Clenching his teeth, Cash elbowed back through the knot of grinning onlookers around them.

"You fat blowhard," skinny, rickety, snow-haired Otis was yelling at Otto.

"You miserable excuse for a wimp," barrel-round, bald Otto was shouting at the same time.

"Gentlemen, gentlemen," Cash began, striving for the genial calm he'd seen his father employ with the two sworn enemies.

"There's but one gentleman here," declared Otis, shaking his bony fist at Otto, "and it ain't you, louse-brain."

Otto's eyeballs bulged above his chipmunk cheeks. "Callin' me a nitwit, are ya, flea-breath?"

Elbowing the two men farther apart, Cash stood his ground. "Now, fellas," he drawled almost as deeply as his father would have. "Let's just calm down here and—"

"Outta my way, sonny," sputtered Otis.

"Let me at 'im," Otto frothed. "I'll show him who's—"

"Chill it!" Cash thundered, pulling them apart as his father would never have done, any more than he'd have raised his voice. "Both of you!"

Otis, Otto and every bystander stepped back and stared openmouthed at him.

"This is your last round together," Cash growled, bracing one hand on each man's heaving chest. "One more and you're both out of here for good. This is *my* market, I'm here to stay, and I make the rules. All you have to do is follow them. Understand?" He drilled both men with a steely glare and repeated, "Understand?"

After swallowing their astonishment, they both gave him sullen half nods of agreement. Then they shuffled off to their respective braided-rug stands, which had faced each other in direct competition for years.

"Big bully," Otto muttered over his shoulder.

"Bully," Otis echoed.

"Thank you, gentlemen." With the testy two in agreement on one point at least, Cash waved a hand to disperse the crowd. "Back to buying and selling and having a good time, folks," he said with an apologetic half smile, then strode off toward the concession building.

Larinda had entered the main gate just in time to witness the fight from beginning to end. She watched the mediator walk away. He was too much of a good thing to ignore, she was thinking. Appraising his height and the breadth of his shoulders—as well as the thickness of his dark hair—she almost sighed, just as she did at the movies when the hero on the screen was a heart-throb.

The surrounding outdoor market scene had its own cinematic quality, colorful and lively with a folksy, small-town crowd of vendors and shoppers. Larinda saw that the flea market offered a wide variety of goods from farm-fresh produce to secondhand hardware.

"Humph. Not *quite* his father, is he, Fran?" a plump woman in her late fifties said.

"Not quite," agreed Fran with a saucy smile, "but I wouldn't kick him out of bed for it, Eva."

Watching his muscled long legs carry him off, Larinda couldn't agree more. Theoretically speaking, of course. As men went, he was fantasy material of the sexiest variety.

But first things first. Had he said this was his market? He, with the dark hair, flint gray eyes and brawny body that had just made noodles of her knees, was Chester? He couldn't be. He was too far from retirement age to be the man she intended to buy out of a lease.

Just to make sure she wasn't imagining things, she edged closer to the two women and asked, "Who was that man in the plaid shirt?"

"Cash Bowman," said Eva, who looked as trim and repressed as her friend looked plump and ready for anything.

"That's his name?" Larinda inquired. "Cash?"

Fran nodded. "He's single, if you're interested," she rushed to add with a toothy grin. "And who wouldn't be interested?"

"Us," Eva said, frowning, "and our husbands."

Fran winked at Larinda. "They can't divorce us for looking, can they? From what I hear," she rattled on, "he's thirty-one, smokes just a little, drinks in moderation, sleeps alone and—"

"Francine Marie!" Eva exclaimed. "Who told you that?"

Looking as smug as her friend looked scandalized, Fran replied, "Your darling single daughter, dearie. Now, where was I? Oh, yes." She pointed to two mobile homes at the edge of the grounds. "And he lives right over there. What else would you like to know about Cash Bowman?"

Larinda had to suppress a smile. "What's his relation to Chester?"

Both women's expressions changed. They looked at each other, then back at Larinda, before responding together in hushed tones, "His son."

Larinda cleared her throat. Something was amiss all of a sudden. But what? "Um, it's Chester I'm looking for. Would you know where can I find him?"

Eva bowed her head. "Six feet deep, God rest him."

"Pardon me?"

"Chester died three weeks ago in an auto accident."

Larinda gulped. "Died?"

"A terrible thing," said Fran. "We're all still missing him here at the market. Always had a smile and a kind word for everyone."

"And the patience of Job with those Purvis brothers," Eva put in, her disapproving frown back in place.

"I . . . see." For a few moments Larinda was silent, stunned by this turn in events.

Larinda had to agree that Cash Bowman had not been patient with the two cantankerous old men. That seemed forgivable, though, if he was still mourning his father. He must be, she reasoned. Having lived through a disaster herself, she could understand that people in mourning were often not themselves. Why, even now, months after losing everything but her life, she wasn't fully herself.

Larinda wrapped her arms around herself in response to a sudden breeze. A wind like this and a light sprinkle of rain were all it took to make her tense. Sometimes she'd get flashbacks to the horrors of the hurricane. She knew the clinical term for it was posttraumatic stress disorder. Unfortunately, knowing the clinical term couldn't help her deal with the urge to panic and run for shelter.

Would she ever be herself again? She shivered and saw Fran's concerned expression. Forcing her arms back down to her sides, she said, "I'm sorry to hear such sad news. I take it that Cash is in charge here now?"

Both women nodded. Then Fran's face lit up again. "He's the only reason all the single women in town show up here every market day. You must be new to Weston."

"I'm just up for the day from Anaheim," Larinda hedged, relieved that the breeze was dying as quickly as it had risen. "I hadn't heard about Chester..."

"Well, if you're interested in seeing Cash, he was headed toward his office in the concession building over there. If you're interested, that is. And who wouldn't be int—"

"For heaven's sake, Fran," Eva scolded, "we came to shop, not to gossip all day. Leave her be." She firmly herded her talkative friend back into the crowd.

"Happy Cash hunting, dear," the irrepressible Fran called over her shoulder. "With that gorgeous red hair of yours, you shouldn't have any trouble."

Larinda watched them go, then gazed around at her inheritance. It was a major disappointment. She hadn't pictured it surrounded by hay fields and small farms. The movie screen was weather ravaged and towered at a forward slant over the crowded market. The fence enclosure sagged and the rows of speaker posts were rusty and bent every which way. It was clear that the Moonglow had seen its last night as a drive-in.

Morey Vito had said in slick, confident tones that it was "somewhat run-down." He had used the same tone the insurance adjuster had used months ago to advise her that a "minor backlog" would delay her claim payment for "just a few days."

Minor backlog. Just a few days. Somewhat rundown. Somewhat?!

Incredulous, she balled her hands into fists and jammed them into the pockets of her flared denim skirt. Couldn't lawyers and insurance companies ever state plain facts? Didn't they even care that human lives and livelihoods were at stake?

As for the attorney's assertion that she could always show movies if Bowman wouldn't budge, it was clear that no viewers could be packed in here, no profit turned without costly repairs—which she couldn't afford. Equally clear and daunting was the flinty determination she had seen in Cash Bowman's eyes and heard in his voice when he'd said this was *his* market and he was here to stay.

Surely, she thought, he couldn't be as determined to stay as she was desperate to sell. If he was, trouble was at hand. How did a property owner go about putting squatters off her property? By legal means, no doubt. Worrisome legal means, and she was sick of worrying. Time-consuming legal means, and she was sick of waiting. *Costly* legal means, and she didn't have a red cent to offer even the cheapest lawyer.

She thought of the little blond boy who had called his father away from the Purvis fracas for a few seconds. There would be more than legalities to consider if the market was Cash Bowman's only livelihood.

It couldn't be, she tried to assure herself. Vito hadn't mentioned anything about anyone but Chester having a principal role at the flea market. But, then, Vito had glossed over a lot of things. The more she discovered, the more she feared another nasty surprise.

Larinda passed a hand wearily under the curly red bangs that shaded her forehead. Perspiration had surfaced there and everywhere else on her body. Her white cotton sweater felt sticky against her skin. Her feet had begun to swell in her knee-high leather boots. She didn't feel at all like the same woman who had barreled down the freeway an hour earlier singing "Happy Days Are Here Again" at the top of her voice. Not the same woman at all.

Before the sun wilted her completely, before her nerve became as scarce as her hope, she started walking quickly toward the concession building. In her canvas shoulder-tote was a copy of the lease. Her only chance for a new start revolved around those few sheets of paper.

Last night, after poring over every word in the document, she had prepared a generous offer contingent on the insurance benefit she was expecting. She'd felt certain Chester Bowman wouldn't refuse.

Now she was certain of nothing—except a deep-down sinking feeling that Chester's son never said anything he didn't mean.

AFTER REACHING the haven of his office, Cash flipped on the desktop air conditioner. Hot under the collar from the unseasonal heat and from the Otis-Otto scuffle, he slumped into what had formerly been his father's desk chair.

It squeaked and groaned under his weight.

Like the secondhand chair, the thirdhand wooden desk and all else in the cramped office, the air conditioner had long since seen its prime. As it sputtered to life, Cash unbuttoned his flannel shirt and waited.

Two minutes later, he was still waiting for cool air to replace the heat wheezing out of the old unit. He fiddled with the temperature knob, then the blower control. Hot, stifling air was all he got.

Swearing, he switched the machine off and tugged off his shirt. Bare to the waist, he sat back and glared out of the security-sealed window behind his desk.

Outside, heat waves shimmied up from the awning over a fruit-vendor's table. California was something else, he reflected. Ninety degrees in the third month of the year. In Oregon, his home state, the snow would be several feet deep.

But he wasn't an Oregon logger now, he reminded himself. He was a Californian. One very hot, very aggravated Californian. The Purvises did it to him every time they butted heads. Until today, though, they hadn't gotten the best of him.

They wouldn't rattle him again, he vowed. Two years from now, after the market had financed his business degree at the local state university, the Purvis brothers could duke it up every day for all he cared. Sure, he liked operating the market in his father's place, but his goal was a business degree, not ulcers from refereeing their boxing matches.

He'd caught Eva Maycomb's comment to Fran as he'd departed the scene. *She's right. I'm not quite my father. If I'd gotten to know him better, I might have been,* he realized regretfully.

A knock sounded on the door, a welcome interruption to his somber thoughts. He checked his watch. *Ten minutes on the nose? No, nine. Good boy, Dan.* Clasping his hands behind his neck, he cocked his feet up on the windowsill and called over the back of the chair, "It's open, Scout."

As the door whooshed open, he winced in anticipation of the loud slam that always punctuated the entrance of his rambunctious seven-year-old son. There was only a faint click. No slam. No feet racing in. No Dan.

"Uh, hello . . . ? Mr. Bowman . . . ?"

The voice behind him was soft and female. Surprised, Cash pushed off from the windowsill and swiveled around in the aged chair. For a moment he was left speechless by the source of that voice. *Hair that red should be illegal on a woman.*

"Uh, hi, I'm Larin—" She stopped, her lips parted, as her eyes focused on his bare chest.

Cash became short of breath and speech failed him a moment longer. *Eyes that big and dark brown should be banned.*

He breathed in with an effort and forced himself to his feet. He could have gaped a lot longer at his unexpected visitor, but he had become conscious of her gaze on his bare torso. He grabbed his shirt and shrugged into it.

"Sorry," he muttered. "The air conditioner's on the blink. What can I do for you?" *Curves like hers should be outlawed.*

"I'm Larinda Outlaw."

Sweet Lord, she's read my mind. No. He'd heard her wrong. Or had he? "Excuse me?"

"Larinda Outlaw," she repeated, and tentatively held out a hand. "Your landlord."

He finished with his last button and slowly wiped his palms down the front of his shirt before he shook her hand. "My what?"

Surprised that he was hard of hearing at thirty-one, Larinda raised her voice. "Well, actually I'm your land*lady*. I've come about the lease." At his quizzical expression, she withdrew her hand from his and said more loudly, "The flea-market lease."

He tugged on his earlobe. "I hear you. What I don't get is—"

"Dad!" Dan called from outside, pounding on the door.

"It's open, Son."

Daniel rushed in, breathless, and let the door slam behind him. "Dad, I'm—" He skidded to a halt when he saw Larinda. "Holy moley," he said, staring at her. "Is that your real hair color?"

Cash winced at the point-blank inquiry. "Er, Dan, it's not polite to—" A wave of his landlady's hand cut him off.

She smiled at Dan. "Yes, it's my real color. Is yours real, too?" she inquired in turn about the boy's flaxen curls.

"Yes, ma'am."

"Holy moley," said Larinda with a conspiratorial wink.

Dan wiggled and giggled. "Hey, Dad. She's neat, huh?"

Cash cleared his throat twice in close succession at that most apt observation. His boy was most definitely a chip off the big block.

"Excuse us for a second," he said to Larinda, and held out his hand to Dan. "How about that key, Scout?"

Larinda watched the boy place it in his father's palm, saw the affectionate glance they shared, and felt strangely excluded from their cozy little family circle.

As if it wasn't enough to be with her own family during the past four months since the hurricane, she'd also begun longing for a husband and children. Right now more than ever. She wasn't her old self.

After all, this man and his son were strangers to her. Dan was a charmer, to be sure, but most children his age were. And if Cash was an eye-catcher as well as a loving father, what of it? The same could be said of more than a few men in this world. She shook off the feeling of longing.

"Thanks again, Dad," Dan said, exchanging a high five with Cash. "Jeffie was mucho impressed."

Cash raised an eyebrow. "Nobody touched the movie projector?"

"'Course not. I promised, remember?"

"Just checking. Want to promise me you'll put some lunch under your belt? Right now."

Daniel's face fell. "Aw, I'd rather polish apples for Mr. Bartley."

"Bartley's apples can wait." Cash pointed at the door. "Lunch. Now."

"What about you? Aren't you gonna eat?"

"I'll catch up with you after I finish with—" He glanced at Larinda. "Are you Miss, Mrs. or Ms.?"

"'Miss' will do."

"After I'm through with Miss Outlaw."

Daniel's jaw dropped and he blinked at Larinda. "Holy moley. Is Outlaw your real name?"

"Daniel J. Bowman," Cash said sternly. "Lunch. Now."

With his head down and his feet dragging, Dan left. He slammed the door louder on his way out than on his way in.

"Kids," said Cash, stuffing his shirt into his pants. "You teach them their manners and what do you get? As I was saying before Dan interrupted . . ." His gaze settled on Larinda Outlaw again. "Holy moley" didn't half describe anything about her. "Uh, let's see now . . . where were we?"

"I've come to discuss the lease arrangement your father has—or *had*—with me." Larinda drew the bound sheaf of papers from her bag and pressed it to her breast as she added, "Regretfully, I never met him. I only learned of his accident a few minutes ago. I'm sorry for your loss."

"Thank you."

Uncomfortable with the subject of death, Larinda continued, "Since I'm the owner of the Moonglow, I—"

"Owner?"

Larinda frowned. He'd had no trouble hearing every word his son had spoken. She raised her voice again. "Yes. Now that I own the Moonglow, I—"

Cash held up a hand. "I'm not going deaf, Miss Outlaw. I hear you, but I find it hard to believe my ears. Jethro Everly owns this property."

"Mr. Bowman, I happen to know your father was notified by registered mail that Jethro left the Moonglow to me in his will." Larinda began fanning her face with the papers in her hand. Nothing was coming easy for her today.

"Will? You mean—" Cash hesitated. "Are you saying Jethro Everly is dead?"

"That can't be news to you after the registered letter his attorney sent," Larinda said. "He told me he called and got no answer. Has your phone been out of order?"

Cash glanced at the ancient telephone next to the worn-out air conditioner. "It had some ringer problems before I got it working again." He frowned. "What letters?"

Larinda sighed and sank into a worn chair. "You don't mind if I sit for a moment, do you?"

"No. Sorry I didn't offer. This ungodly heat." Cash backed down into his own chair and regarded her over the scratched desktop. "Look, I have no knowledge of Jethro's death or any registered letter or change of ownership on the Moonglow. And to my knowledge, neither did my father."

Hearing that, Larinda began fanning her face hard enough to lift her bangs off her forehead. "Whatever the case, Mr. Bowman, I've inherited the Moonglow. You see, Jethro was my godfather."

"Join the club. He was mine, too," said Cash.

Larinda ceased fanning herself. Her bangs flopped against her damp forehead.

"Hard man to figure," Cash commented, then added, "for a godfather, I mean. I wouldn't know him from Adam if he walked in right now. Would you?"

"No. He never did anything godfatherly—until now."

Cash sighed. "Well, he did something nice for me, as well, recently. Without the market, I'd be up a tall tree without safety boots right now." He eyed her over the desk. "So he was godfather to both of us. And now you're my landlady."

"No, Mr. Bowman. I'm your—"

"'Cash,' Larinda. I do business on a first-name basis." He leaned back in his chair. "What do you mean by no?"

Larinda resumed fanning herself. "I mean I'm your *father's* landlady, Cash, not yours. In the event of his death before lease end, all rights to the property revert to me. Again, I regret his passing," she hastened to add, "but the terms of this lease are quite clear." She pushed it across the desk to him.

He scanned it. "The terms of my lease amendment are even clearer. I don't see it attached."

"What amendment?"

Cash opened a desk drawer and pulled out a file folder. "This one. It names me the lessee in the event of my father's disability or death."

2

STUNNED, Larinda stared across the desk at Cash. "Are you serious?"

"About what?"

"This—this amendment to the lease."

"Sure. Why would I joke about a thing like that?"

"You have an amendment."

"Right here," he confirmed, tapping the file with his index finger.

"An amendment signed by Jethro?"

"Of course. What good would it be unsigned?"

"May I see it?"

He handed it over. As Larinda scanned it she had to strive for inner and outer calm. "There must be some mistake, Mr. Bowman. The will cleared probate. According to the estate attorney, no liens other than the lease I brought with me apply to my property."

"No mistake," Cash contended. "Whether he had a premonition or what, my father requested this amendment a few months before his accident—and Jethro agreed."

Larinda examined the document more closely, her fingers shaking. It was indeed an amendment to the original lease. It had been notarized and the signatures were those of Jethro, Chester and a third party as witness.

"This just can't be." She lifted her eyes from the last page to meet Cash's quizzical gray gaze. "If you were aware of this, why didn't you advise Jethro's attorney of it after you got his letter?"

Cash frowned. "Listen, aside from the fact that I don't know anything about any letter, I'm not responsible for notifying anyone of changes in the leases Jethro signed. That was his business, not mine or my father's. Frankly, I can't see what you're so flustered about. What difference does it make if you're my father's landlady or mine?"

Larinda opened her mouth to enlighten him on the world of difference it made, then snapped it shut. She hadn't run a successful business in the past without learning how to finesse a deal. She had learned that the less said before negotiating any terms, the better.

She had to calm down. If Cash knew she was desperate to sell, he'd drive a harder bargain than he might otherwise. If he had a head for business, that was. And the way her luck had run ever since the hurricane, he was probably as hardheaded and shrewd as they came.

"Difference?" She settled back in her chair. "No difference, as long as the rent gets paid."

"I'm current and I'll stay that way. What other guarantees do you need to stop looking so red in the face?"

"None. It's this heat. I can't help wondering, though, why your father never got that registered letter."

Cash shrugged. "For all I know, he did. I've only been here a month. To be honest, I haven't gone through his things yet. There are boxes stacked up in the trailer, waiting, but with getting Dan into school here and learning the flea-market business by the seat of my pants, well . . ." He spread his hands in appeal. "I'll get around to it."

By the seat of his pants, hmm? Larinda thought. A glimmer of hope flickered. "You've never operated a flea market before?" she inquired.

Cash shook his head. "Until a month ago, I was an unemployed Oregon logger." He directed a faraway look out the window. "The environmental laws protecting the northern spotted owl haven't done the timber industry any favors. Now loggers are as endangered as those damned owls are."

"How did you end up here?"

"My father got in touch and invited me to move down and work with him." He stared outside a moment longer, then back at Larinda. "You know, I didn't expect to like running a flea market, but I do. I like it better than logging. And God knows, I need the job right now as much as it needs me."

This Larinda didn't need to hear. His words hit home, straight to her heart. Loss of any kind, caused by an act of God or an environmental freeze on logging, she could identify with all too readily. And sympathize with, too.

She shifted in her chair, uncomfortable with her role as Ebenezer Scrooge. Hardhearted had never been her style. Hardworking, fair, willing to iron things out, *that* was her style. Her former employees could attest to it, for she had paid them well and never asked of them anything she hadn't asked first of herself. Applying that rule, she hadn't often gone wrong in business or in life.

However, she wasn't sure how to apply it to the problem fate was posing for her in Cash Bowman. From the way he had described them, his own straits sounded dire enough. He apparently hadn't done anything to inflict them on himself except to be in the wrong place at the wrong time. Nevertheless, she reminded herself, her own straits were dire, too. If he was broke through no fault of his own...well, so was she. Still, she couldn't help feeling that her intentions were pretty Scrooge-like as she returned his gaze.

His eyes were beautiful, she suddenly thought. Gray with deep blue flecks. They blinked once, in slow motion, as she looked into them. It would be difficult to play hardball with someone whose eyes reflected such honesty and sincerity.

"I know how it feels to have little to go on," she found herself blurting out, despite every good reason she had to conceal the information. "I lost my business and belongings recently. Everything."

Cash leaned forward, concerned. "How?"

"Hurricane."

"The one in Texas last fall?"

She nodded and, before he could react, went on, "In the past week I've gone from owning nothing to owning the Moonglow. I need to sell it as soon as possible to get back on my feet. If your amendment is authentic, I'm prepared to make you a fair buy-out offer on the lease."

After a short span of silence, he said, "Do you happen to have a husband? Kids to support?"

"Neither."

"None to support or none, period?"

"None at all. I—"

"You've got a bed to sleep in?"

She detected the cooling edge in his tone and got his drift. She matched her tone to his. "The sofa bed in my parents' living room in Anaheim."

"You also have two mobile homes on your property here," he asserted, "one of which is mine to live in under the terms of the lease. As for the other, it's all yours. There's nothing to prevent you from moving into it right now if you want your own personal bed."

Larinda returned his frosty smile. "That's all well and good, but I have a new business to start up and a living to make elsewhere."

"Where?"

"I'm not sure yet. Near my parents, I hope. The population density has to be right."

"For what?"

"Outlaw Home Video, with a specialty in Westerns. To finance it, I have to sell this place right away. I'm prepared to offer you a fair price."

"And where am I supposed to go with your fair price?"

"Wherever you'd rather be. You won't be leaving the Moonglow empty-handed."

"Fair price or unfair price, I won't be leaving the Moonglow period."

"But you don't know what I'm offering yet."

"I don't need to. Since I got here, I've come up with several ideas to increase the profit this market brings in. In twelve months I'll be in more decent financial shape than I'd be now if I sold out to you. In another twelve months I'll complete my small-business classes at Weston College. Selling out right now wouldn't get me what I want."

"How can you be certain of that," Larinda retorted, "when I haven't said what I'm willing to pay?"

"Say it."

She named a price.

"No," he said.

She named a second, higher, amount.

"No dice."

She named a third, the highest she could go, a price Chester Bowman would have snapped up in a second, she was sure.

"Very tempting, but my lease is not for sale" was his son's answer. "This time next year it's yours by law, but until then it's mine."

Larinda pulled her chair closer. "If you haven't noticed, that third, very generous, offer was my *final* offer."

"I figured that out before I refused." Cash nodded knowingly. "Any higher and you'd be losing your shirt."

"Yet your answer remains no?"

"No, it is, and no, it stays." He stood and looked down at her. "I have a son to support and a roof to keep over his head as well as mine. I also have schooling to complete. If I was as single as you are and didn't need this ticket to the future, I'd take the money and run, but right now I'm not a man with anywhere to run to."

"Look, Mr. Bowman—"

"'Cash.'"

Larinda set her jaw. "Cash." Oh, what she wouldn't do for the real thing. Cash, ready cash, enough to start over again. Not this man who was blocking her every move. Cash. A misnomer for sure.

Slowly, she stood and faced him for one last try. "What I'd like to do is forget your last no and discuss this further over dinner tonight. Are you free?"

"My answer will be the same after dessert."

Determined that she could come up with an argument to sway him, she repeated, "Are you free or not?"

"Not if I can't get a sitter for Dan between now and then."

"What are your chances of getting one?"

"Nil. I don't even know one. I'm not big on dating and needing sitters."

So Fran was right, she thought before she persisted, "Perhaps Dan would like to join us, then."

"Are you always this pushy, Larinda?"

"Only when I'm backed up against a wall. Are you always this stubborn, Cash?"

"Only when *I'm* backed up against a wall. May I offer a solution to the stalemate?"

"Certainly. I'm willing to negotiate."

"Negotiating isn't what I have in mind. My solution is that you move into the other trailer and get a job in Weston for a year. At the end of it you can do anything you want with this place."

"That's bright," she agreed, "but not a fraction as bright as *my* idea of selling the Moonglow and having what I want now."

He stuck his chin out. "All things considered, you're not as hard up as I am. You could take out a loan with the property as collateral."

"I've been in debt before," she informed him, "and I'm not jumping back in if I can help it."

He regarded her, unmoved. "Sorry I can't offer you my shoulder to cry on. You have options I don't have, like working in town as I said and living here rent-free. Plus, you own this property. It won't stop being worth something after a year is up. That's more than I can say for my lease. I need my year more than you need to sell."

"But—"

"Forget the buts." He cut her off firmly. "Now that my lease won't be renewed as I'd planned, I'm damned well going to make the most of the time I have left."

Larinda felt her last flicker of hope die out in the face of his inarguable logic and undeniable need. Hot tears threatened at the corners of her eyes. It was clear from his stubborn tone that a good meal would not soften Cash up. As determined as she might be, she would be wasting the little money she had.

"Will you at least give me a tour of my drive-in before I leave, Cash?"

He nodded obligingly, but his determined expression didn't alter one bit. He was here to stay for twelve long months. She wouldn't be putting For Sale signs up on the battered movie screen this afternoon as she had planned.

She'd just be driving back to L.A. singing "Nobody Knows The Trouble I've Seen."

TWO HOURS LATER, instead of being Anaheim-bound, Larinda stood in the Moonglow parking lot and stared into the greasy rear engine of her father's VW van.

In twenty years, the trusty vehicle had never suffered a breakdown. It had waited until today. Now, no moving part she jiggled or wiggled in the engine made it start when she turned the key and pressed the gas pedal. She closed her weary eyes and cursed under her breath. She refrained from shouting by biting down hard on her lower lip.

As if everything else hadn't been enough. Now this. After an appalling tour with Cash of her decrepit inheritance, after a bitter repeat of their initial argument over the lease—this.

She needed a tow truck. Fishing in her tote for a quarter, she stomped back through the thinning flea-market crowd to the pay phones in the small concession building. There were only two of them, both a few feet from Cash's closed office door, both in use. She folded her arms and tapped a toe.

Ten minutes later, she was still tapping and ready to explode, when Cash came barreling out of his office. He halted in mid-step when he saw her. "I thought you left."

"I tried." She glared at the two bubble-gum chewing preteens monopolizing the phones. "I need a tow truck. The van won't start."

"Won't go or won't start?"

Only a man, she thought, would make such a pointlessly fine distinction. It only added fuel to the fire that he was also the man with whom she'd parted an hour ago on uncongenial terms.

"All I need is a tow truck, thank you."

Cash eyed her greasy fingernails and cuticles. "You tried to fix it yourself?"

"No," she said with a facetious smile, "this is the newest craze in manicures. Low-tech."

"Very funny, Red. Is it the new look in noses, too?"

Red. She had never loathed a nickname more than that one. His choice only proved his immense lack of imagination. *Red.* She was beginning to see it. It took all her powers of self-restraint not to wipe the smudge off her nose with the sleeve of her sweater. Never had a man seemed more insufferable to her than he did at that moment.

"Give me your keys and I'll take a look at it," Cash said, seemingly unaware of her dangerous mood.

"Never call me 'Red,'" she warned.

"Whatever you say, Red." He smirked. "I know a fair share about VW engines. Do you want me to take a look at it or not?"

Larinda gritted her teeth so hard her gums hurt. "I said I'm calling a tow truck."

His glanced at the two prattling youths. "Not anytime soon you aren't."

She swallowed, then inquired with exaggerated politeness, "May I use *your* phone, then? Pretty please?"

"Sure." He smirked again and opened his office door for her. "Why didn't you ask in the first place?"

She considered spitting back *Why didn't you offer in the first place?* but thought better of it. She stormed through the door. It would be wiser to arrange for a tow truck before shredding his smug jaw with her low-tech claws.

AN HOUR LATER she was standing with a grease-covered mechanic in a garage ten miles from the Moonglow. "Four hundred dollars and two days to fix what's wrong?" she asked in disbelief.

"One day," the mechanic corrected. "Tomorrow's Sunday. We don't fix on Sundays. Monday's the soonest we can get to her."

"But four *hundred* dollars?"

His reply was a nonchalant innocent shrug. "You want her fixed or not?"

"But where am I going to get the—" Larinda closed her eyes. This on top of everything else. What choice did she have? "Do it. Fix her."

He smiled. "You need a courtesy ride somewhere?"

"That would help."

"Where?"

It was a long moment before she could mutter, "Back to the Moonglow Drive-in."

"BACK SO SOON?" Cash inquired, when Larinda entered his office for the third time that day.

She sank into the same worn chair and mentally cursed the heat. As the sun set, the air was cooling off outside, but inside it was still stifling.

"I won't be driving home today," she told him tersely.

He nodded. "I figured you wouldn't."

"I'll be staying here. Any objections?"

"No. You own the place if I recall correctly."

On their tour, Cash had shown her through the two mobile homes in the far corner of the property. His was a roomy, comfortable two-bedroom. The other was one bedroom and had been the movie manager's quarters. It had seen better days.

"If you can spare a sheet and blanket for the night, I'd appreciate it."

A corner of his mouth twitched. "I've spared both—and made up the bed just in case."

"Why, thank you," she said after an instant of total surprise.

"You're welcome. When *will* you be driving home?"

"Monday, if they're telling me the truth."

"How much to repair it?"

"Too much. My father's wiring the money. The van's his. I'll repay him for his trouble somehow, someday." She met Cash's level gaze across the desk. "I maxed out my only credit card with the tow-truck charge. Can I beg dinner tonight and pay you back later?"

A wisp of a smile curved his lips. "I just happen to be free," he said. "Dan got a last-minute invitation to spend the night at Jeffie's house. How does candlelight and fine wine sound after a rough day?"

"I'm imagining something I can pay back sooner, like a TV dinner."

"TV dinner," he chided, looking offended. "I'm a better Samaritan than that. It's my treat tonight, Red."

"But I—"

He held up a hand. "My treat."

"Okay. Thanks again." She was too tired and dispirited to argue—except on one final point. "Cash, I don't want to sound ungrateful, but would you stop this 'Red' business? I'm not Katharine Hepburn and you're not Cary Grant and this is not *The Philadelphia Story*."

"What's *The Philadelphia Story*?"

"Surely you've seen it. The movie?"

He shrugged. "I'm neutral on movies. They come, they go."

Neutral. Larinda had to exert extra effort not to roll her eyes. Who could be neutral about movies? However, discovering that Cash wasn't in the know was a positive thing. One more thing to detract from the attraction she'd felt toward him from the start.

"It's a classic 1940 romantic comedy," she explained. "One where everything goes wrong—like it did today. Only today was no comedy."

"Where does 'Red' fit into it?"

"Hepburn plays a rich, spoiled redhead who hates the nickname," she told him. "Grant plays her suave ex-husband who uses it whenever he can for obvious reasons."

"To crisp her, you mean."

"Exactly."

"That wasn't my intent, exactly."

"Whatever your intention, I can do without 'Red.'"

"Even if it was meant as a salute?"

"To what?"

"Your spirit."

She sat, surprised into silence again.

"And to your hair," he added. "It's spectacular, like a forest fire in the night. I helped fight a few up in Oregon, so I know."

The way Cash's gaze lingered on her face and hair caused Larinda's heart to miss a beat. She couldn't look away from his gray, piercing eyes. Even when she noted a flash of raw, sexual awareness in them, she couldn't break their locked gaze. Men had eyed her in that way before. She had always been able to look up or down or sideways at will before, no matter how compelling the man. Cash's eyes took hold and didn't let go.

She became aware that she was flashing her own sexual awareness of Cash back at him. But her attempt to break free failed. He held her visually captive a moment longer and then Daniel, her savior, burst in.

"Jeffie's mom's out front in the car," he announced, swinging a duffel bag from one hand. He looked at Larinda. "Hi. I get to sleep at Jeffie's overnight. Neat, huh?"

Cash stood up and rounded the desk. "Did you pack your toothbrush, Son?"

"Yep."

"Toothpaste? Pajamas?"

"Dad," the boy protested, "I know what to take for overnight. I'm not a little kid anymore."

"Are you too grown up to give your old dad a good-bye hug before you go?"

"Nah. 'Bye, Dad." Dan threw his arms around his father's long legs and hid his face.

Larinda watched Cash cup his son's tousled blond head and felt the same sudden longing she had felt earlier. These yearnings for domesticity had to stop, she told herself. She wasn't the missing female element in the Bowman family tableau.

It disturbed her that she was mentally linking herself with Cash and Dan. She turned away from them and looked out the window to where dusk was gathering over the market. This second time the longing was harder to brush off.

"I'll walk you out, Scout," Cash said. He turned to Larinda. "Join us?"

Wary of meeting his eyes again, she kept hers where they were. "I'll wait here, thanks."

"Is Mrs. Outlaw's name *really* Outlaw?" she heard Dan inquire as they went out.

"'Miss,' Dan, not 'Mrs.,'" Cash corrected.

"Gee, you mean you could marry her?"

The door closed. Larinda sat in the sudden silence and closed her eyes, thinking that Dan was lucky to be so oblivious. After her last failed romance, Larinda had decided to steer clear of involvements. She couldn't let herself forget that decision.

As much as her parents were dying to be grandparents, marriage and motherhood weren't in her personal plan. No, she wouldn't be changing Outlaw to any married name. She'd had too many disappointments with men. Besides, she liked her name.

Not that it wasn't a trial to be named Outlaw. Making dinner reservations, plane reservations, any reservations with a name like hers was no breeze. How many maître d's and airline agents had she watched suppress a smile as she gave her name.

It was only when she had named her video store after herself that Outlaw had come into its own as a genius of a name for a store with a specialty in Westerns. Outlaw Home Video. It had been perfect. That she could point out her parents' names, Larry and Linda Outlaw, in the credits of *Wild West* was the crowning touch.

Larinda smiled, remembering how she had grown up begging her parents to switch back from Outlaw to Smith. Request denied. "Jethro Everly was right," her father had patiently explained. "No one ever forgets a name like Outlaw." To which her mother had always added, "It goes with your hair, Larinda. Smith doesn't."

"Right, Mom," Larinda now murmured. She ran her fingers through the thick, glossy mass of her hair from her temples to where it tumbled over her shoulders to mid-back. A year ago, she had been halfway serious about a long, tall Texan who had a preference for short hair. She sighed. The length of her hair hadn't been their only conflict in tastes and attitudes.

Her thoughts roamed from him to Cash. Long or short hair? Which was his preference? She pictured his fingers weaving through her crowning glory with sex-

ual intent. She could almost feel him lifting the mass of
it off her neck from behind and lowering his mouth to
the warm skin he'd bared.

"Spectacular," she recalled his saying earlier. "Like a
forest fire in the night."

The vivid image he'd conjured up suggested he had
a powerful visual sense. It explained why he had looked
at her earlier with such intensity. As a visually percep-
tive man, he would study a person at length with his
eyes. As a lover, he would—

She stopped the thought and any further speculation, as well. Her experiences with men, few and far
between, had never been romantic on the grand scale
of *Dr. Zhivago* or *Casablanca*. More than anything, she
reflected, they'd been minor tragedies that had taught
her how rarely men were true romance heroes.

Accidentally finding her man in bed with another
woman had been a major deterrent to trusting men.
When she'd finally taken a chance on another relationship, she'd been betrayed once more. She wasn't willing to place her trust in any man again.

It had been a long time since she had been sexual with
a man except in fantasy. As harmless as it might seem,
this was not the place or time to imagine Cash as a
trustworthy lover feasting his lucent gray gaze on every
inch of her body. He could walk back in at any moment. He did.

Bolting up from her chair, she saw that he wasn't
alone. With him was a stocky, gray-haired man in a security officer's uniform.

"Walt Whitman," Cash said, "meet the new landlady, Larinda Outlaw."

Walt grinned. "If you won't ask how I got named after a poet," he said, shaking Larinda's hand, "I won't ask how you got named after Jesse James."

"It's a deal," Larinda agreed, liking him at once.

"Walt's retired from the sheriff's department," Cash explained. "He works night security here and oversees the cleanup crew."

Walt jingled a ring of keys. "Time to start locking a few things up. You two through in here?"

Cash nodded and led Larinda out of the office. "The place is all yours, Walt."

Leaving him to secure the concession building, they walked through the almost-deserted flea-market area. A few vendors were still packing up, preparing to call it a day.

"A fine mess we have here," she remarked as she and Cash sidestepped litter left and right. "Who cleans up?"

"A couple of college kids from town. They work fast. Things'll be shipshape pretty soon." Cash glanced sideways at her. "Clean enough to show movies, if you wanted to."

"If I had money to burn," she said, "I might be interested. Without it, I'm not."

"Good," he said. "I like it this way. With you showing movies, I'd have to close earlier and take a cut in concession profits as a result. Everything would be a scramble at sundown." He halted and looked up at the dark hulk of the movie screen against the sunset-tinged sky. "It's sad, though, that drive-ins are a dying breed. My folks used to pile my brother and me into the car every so often in the summer and haul us off to one of these for a family flick."

Larinda smiled. "Mine, too. Summer wasn't summer without drive-in movies."

"It sure wasn't summer without them when I was sixteen," Cash said, the tilt of his smile wolfish. "Those were the days, if you ask me. A summer night, a willing girl, a drive-in movie—better known as The Passion Pit. What more could a high-school kid want?"

"Only what he went there for," she teased. "How many of those drive-in movies did you ever really watch?"

Cash chuckled. "That was their great charm. They didn't have to be watched to be enjoyed. How many did *you* actually catch a glimpse of?" he teased back.

"I wasn't that kind of girl."

"What kind were you?"

She pursed her lips. "The kind who watched most of the movie and left the boy sulking in the driver's seat."

"*Most* of the movie?"

"I didn't rule out a few kisses."

"I remember girls like you back then," Cash taunted. "A challenge."

"I remember boys like you back then," Larinda returned. "A threat."

They laughed together at that, then walked on. He had a nice laugh, she decided, and an engaging sense of humor. Just as nice was the thoughtfulness he had shown by readying a bed for her. Even more kind was his offer of candlelight and fine wine at dinner to ease the awful day she'd had.

Considering all that, she knew she'd do well to bear in mind what he'd been in his youth. Once a back-seat bad boy, always a back-seat bad boy.

At the door of mobile home, he said, "I put in soap and towels for you. Anything else you need?"

"No. Give me a half hour and I'll be myself again."

"Okay, I'll be back in thirty and we'll be off."

Alone inside her trailer, Larinda looked around more closely than she had earlier that day. Living area furnished in earth-tone stripes. Compact kitchen. Full bath. Cash hadn't stinted in making the double bed, she observed in the bedroom. Floral-print spread. Fat pillows.

She bounced her hand on the bed before lying down to test the mattress. A good one, she thought, firm with just enough give for comfort. She lay there, relieved. *My own bed,* she thought. Not the brass one she had slept in before the hurricane had twisted it into scrap metal, but still a bed of her own.

She let her head sink into a pillow and stared up at the ceiling. *My own roof.* Not the peaked roof she had once slept under, but still a roof of her own. Not the four papered walls of the bedroom she had once dreamed sweet, secure dreams in, but still four walls that belonged to her.

She thought of how independent she'd been before the hurricane—and how dependent she'd been ever since. It pained her that the disaster had forced her to rely on public charity before leaving Texas and on family charity after her return home. Though her parents would cheerfully help out as long as necessary, they couldn't afford it.

Each handout had eroded her self-esteem. She'd taken personal pride in supporting herself with her own business.

It felt good now to own something that wasn't a relief handout or a charitable contribution. She smiled. It would feel twice as good to be self-employed at Outlaw Video II after talking Cash out of his lease over dinner.

"Wherever you are," Larinda whispered, "thank you, Jethro Everly."

3

CASH HAD SHOWERED, shaved and was ready for the evening of candlelight and wine he'd promised Larinda. He knocked on her door thirty minutes after he'd left her. There was no response. He knocked a second time and waited. It could only mean one thing, he decided, which boiled down to one word.

Women. Just as his ex-wife would have been late right now after agreeing to be ready, Larinda was probably still lingering in the shower. He'd have to twiddle his thumbs while she got her eye shadow just right. Yawn while she fooled with her face powder and her nail polish. Lord knows he'd spent enough time waiting for Rita to know how long a woman could take before she was ready to go out.

The only things Rita hadn't delayed were getting pregnant and deciding after he married her that she preferred bright lights and big cities to motherhood and marriage. That had been fine with Cash. Two years of waiting had been his limit. The last he had heard she was living it up in Paris with a jet-set playboy. Women.

Cash knocked a third time, then scowled at the door. Larinda Outlaw hadn't seemed vain. She'd worn her wildfire hair spilling over her shoulders and a minimum of makeup. Looks were evidently misleading.

He tried the doorknob. When he found it unlocked, he stepped inside. Lights were on in the living room and kitchen. He ventured a step down the short hall and saw that the bathroom door was open and the space within was dark. At the end of the hall, light shone through the open bedroom door.

"Knock-knock. Anybody home?" No answer. "I'm here." Cash waited for a response. When it didn't come, he approached the bedroom door. "Larinda? You in there?"

He leaned around the doorjamb and saw that his landlady was out like a light. She obviously hadn't meant to fall asleep before dinner. It was a rare woman who settled down for a nap fully clothed with knee-high leather boots on. He eased in and stood looking down at her. She lay flat on her back, her arms and legs spread-eagled on the bedspread. Her lips were slightly open as though she were sighing blissfully.

Cash roamed a slow gaze over her. Her hair made a fiery shape against the white pillow. The top of her head came to his shoulder when she was standing, but now she seemed smaller, fragile, eminently feminine—and sexy in a way he couldn't overlook.

Cash watched the gentle rise and fall of her breasts under her white sweater. They were curves a man couldn't ignore. He wouldn't hesitate for a second to take their measure under the right circumstances. Her slender waist and hips looked just as alluring as her slim legs under her long denim skirt.

His gaze caught in the arrowed valley her skirt formed between her upper thighs and he remembered her confirming earlier, "Yes, it's my real hair color." He'd been wondering ever since if that held true over her whole body.

At the intriguing possibility that it did, he let a long, silent whistle pass his lips. They felt hot, as hot as his physical arousal. It had been some time since a woman had affected him this way. Larinda Outlaw had been doing it from the instant she had walked into his office.

No question of that or of what he wasn't going to do about it. Resisting temptation would be the smart thing, he'd already decided, even though his body clearly had other ideas. *It* might be ready to get personal with Larinda, but *he* wasn't. Despite the appeal her spirited personality had begun to hold for him, her goals remained as opposed to his as his ex-wife's had been.

Cash thought back on how much he'd learned about conflict and opposition. He didn't need a refresher course from Larinda. It was a good thing she'd be leaving on Monday.

"WHAT . . . ?"

Larinda had been startled awake by the sound of a slamming door. For a moment she couldn't identify where she was or what time it was. She squinted at the curtained window. An aura of pale light rimmed the curtains. Dawn.

Memory rushed in and she lay back. She was at the Moonglow. She'd apparently fallen asleep and slept all night. In her boots. She wiggled her toes.

Snapping on the bedside lamp, she surveyed her present situation. Who had covered her with a thick down sleeping bag? Who else but her only neighbor. It must have been the slam of his door that had awakened her.

Knowing that Cash had found her asleep made her cringe. It had been so long since she'd slept with anyone in her bedroom that she wondered if she snored and didn't know it. If so, she hated to think that Cash might know.

"Maybe he snores, too," she muttered, and sat up to kick off her boots. "What do I care what he knows?"

The truth was that she cared more than she was comfortable admitting. As stubborn and unyielding as Cash could be, he was also the sort of man a woman didn't run into every day. The sort she now had to wish hadn't been nice enough to make her bed and cover her with his sleeping bag. For it had to be his. It smelled like a man and made her want to share it with a man who smelled just like that.

She stood, both to escape that evocative male scent and to get the blood in her feet moving again. Before she could move, however, she heard the front door to her new abode click open. She detected the sound of stealthy footsteps in her kitchen.

"Who's there?"

Whoever it was replied with an unintelligible grunt. Then she heard a dull thud followed by a resounding *pop!* That was enough for Larinda to grab up one of her boots and ready it for anything.

"Cash? Is that you?"

Another grunt was the reply, as unintelligible as the first. Since she couldn't identify the voice as Cash's, she planned a surprise offense. Brandishing her boot, heel out, she would bash the intruder to a pulp.

She rushed into the kitchen and found a champagne bottle on the kitchen floor gushing white foam all over Cash Bowman's worn Reeboks.

"Hllmmnfff," he grunted around the stems of three red plastic roses that were clamped between his teeth.

His hands had obviously been too full of candles and candleholders for him to keep a grip on the bottle now at his feet. He squished through the foaming wine to the kitchen counter and put down what he held.

Removing the roses from between his teeth, he turned and gave her a dark look of reproach. "You aren't supposed to be awake."

Larinda lowered her weapon and backed away from the spreading tide of champagne. "I wouldn't be if someone hadn't slammed a door."

"It wasn't supposed to slam," he said.

"What are you doing here, Cash?"

"Making good on a promise." He swept a hand dispiritedly at the floor and the counter. "Last night I promised you candlelight and fine wine. This morning I thought I could sneak in, leave this stuff here and sneak out. Don't ask why, but I wanted what I promised last night to be here when you woke up this morning."

"But . . . why?"

He threw up his hands. "Say don't ask and she asks." He tiptoed past her into the bathroom and came out with two thick bath towels. After spreading them out to soak up the champagne, he straightened to face her.

"I did it because I feel sorry for you, Larinda. No one deserves a hurricane. I wish I could end your problems by taking your offer. I would if I could, but I can't."

"Cash, you—"

His upraised hand cut her short. "I'm not through. These candles and cheap bubbly were just to let you know you've got a rain check for a nice dinner whenever you want it. I figured you'd wake up and see the stuff and get the message. But I blew it." He turned and stalked out the door.

Larinda watched it swing shut after him, her mouth gaping open. She switched her attention from the door to the towels on the floor. Blew it? He'd done no such thing. She appreciated his thoughtfulness.

But she couldn't ignore that he'd said he felt sorry for her. In that respect he *had* blown it. Being pitied ranked right up there with being called "Red." His or anyone else's pity she could do without just fine, thank you. She dropped to her knees and finished the mop-up job.

After she'd cleaned up the mess and taken a shower, it occurred to her what scorning his pity would mean. She wouldn't get breakfast or a ride to Western Union to collect the funds her father had said he'd wire by noon today. At this point, both were essential.

She'd gone without lunch yesterday, and dinner last night, so she was now famished. Without the Red Cross kitchen to sustain her as it had in Texas, she had the choice of dining on her pride or appealing to Cash's pity.

She chose Cash. Leaving her trailer, she went to his door and knocked.

He answered it at the first knock. "How do you like your eggs?" he asked before she could open her mouth to beg.

"However you like to cook them."

"They're scrambled this morning, like the champagne. Come in." He led her inside and pulled out a chair for her at the kitchen table. "Have a seat. Coffee? Cream, sugar . . . ?"

Larinda, who would have drunk toxic waste at that point, nodded. "Black, please."

He filled an oversize cup for her, then popped bread into the toaster before he turned to the stove where butter was melting in a frying pan. "Sorry I left you with that mess," he said, his back to her. "I was too mad at myself to finish the job."

"I . . . I appreciate your rain check, Cash. And I'm sorry I have to beg breakfast from you, so we're both sorry about something." She had to force herself to add, "While I'm begging, may I borrow your car to get to Western Union later today?"

"Sure." Cash glanced at her over his shoulder. "Better a help than a hindrance, I always say. The last thing I need is to run myself any further afoul of my landlady."

Larinda sipped her coffee. "You're not afoul of me."

"Since when? I'm the guy who won't take your fair price and run, remember? The one who nicknamed you 'Red' yesterday and crisped you good. How much further on the wrong side of a landlady can a guy get?"

She shrugged. "I haven't been a landlady long enough to know."

"You couldn't have a better man leasing from you, I guarantee that," Cash claimed, wielding a spatula. "I'm honest and conscientious. You'll find things in good shape the day I leave—the things I'm responsible for, that is. The fence, the screen and the speaker posts, well, they're not my territory."

Larinda sipped more coffee. "I wish they weren't mine, either. I wish they were . . ."

He glanced over his shoulder again. "I know. You wish it were all sold with the proceeds going to Outlaw Video."

"You don't have to make me sound so self-serving." Annoyed, she set her coffee cup down with a thump. "Owning my own video store is the only work experience I've had except for my parents' deli. Can you blame me for wishing?"

"I knew nothing but logging until recently. Who am I to blame you? But remember that environmentalists and the northern spotted owl have put a lot of loggers like me out of business. Hurricanes aren't the only wish busters out there. For one reason or another, many people have to learn new survival skills."

Larinda fixed his back with a chilly stare. "In a year I'm going to sell this place and regain the financial security I had before the hurricane. That doesn't require new survival skills."

"How much financial security are you after?"

"Enough to never worry like my parents did when I was young about keeping a roof over the family's head and food in the refrigerator. After the bank repossessed the car, we depended on welfare for a while," she said with a catch in her voice. "I never want to trade in a food stamp again."

"Are your parents any better off now?"

She nodded. "They finally got it together when they stopped being starving actors and started up a delicatessen. It pays their bills. That's about all."

"How did you finance the video store you lost?"

"By pinching pennies while I managed it. The owner sold it for a pittance in her divorce dispute."

"How do you figure to survive for the next twelve months?"

I don't know," she replied. As she watched him buttering toast, Larinda was reminded of the kindness he had extended to her. And here she had been snapping at him, an ungrateful charity case.

In a warmer tone, she continued. "I'll probably go on working in the deli as I did through college. As I've done since I left Texas."

"But how long can you go on sleeping on the sofa in your parents' living room?"

"My brother has launched a campaign to trade his room for the sofa. Larson is eighteen and trying to be a knight in shining armor to his poor, old homeless sister."

"Not so old compared to me at thirty-one," Cash commented. "What are you, twenty-five?"

"Twenty-eight. Too old to be living at home. My insurance money will solve that. It's due any day now— I hope. Hope's all I have to go on for the time being."

"Give hope a rest. Try going on this, instead." Cash set a plate of eggs and toast in front of her and a plate of the same for himself across the table. He refilled their coffee cups and sat down. Instead of picking up his fork and digging in, however, he just sat there.

Larinda looked up from her plate. "What?"

"Your hair. Where did you get that red?"

She self-consciously touched a strand of it. "From my mother's side of the family. My father's is brown—he's losing it fast. And my brother's is somewhere in between."

"Where are your brown eyes from?"

"Ask the gene experts. My father's are brown, my mother's and brother's are blue."

Cash picked up his fork. "It's an arresting combination."

"Thank you . . . I think."

"I wouldn't have said it if I didn't mean it as a compliment. And don't thank me again, for anything. Especially for breakfast. No need to."

"I owe you. I'll pay you back," Larinda said firmly, cutting into her eggs.

He raised his eyebrows in visible reproach. "Haven't you ever done anything charitable without expecting to be repaid?"

"Of course I have. But I like it a lot better on the giving end."

"Seems to me it goes both ways. 'Bread cast upon the waters,' et cetera."

"What bread I've cast has already come back to me tenfold. After I boarded up my shop and living quarters, I only had enough time to pack a toothbrush before the hurricane strike area was evacuated. She plucked at her sleeve. "See this sweater? Red Cross. My skirt? Salvation Army. My boots? A department-store donation. My—"

Cash held up both hands. "Okay, I get the message. You've had it with handouts and helping hands—including mine."

She gave him a small, tight smile and returned to stabbing at her eggs. "As I said, I'll be paying you back. I don't know when, but I will."

Cash looked at her long and hard. "How about starting bright and early this morning?"

"This morning? How?" She stopped her fork halfway between her plate and her mouth.

"Sunday's my busiest day. Help me get everyone checked in this morning and you'll earn your keep until the van's back on the road again. Okay?"

She couldn't reply fast enough. "When do I start?"

"After you've had seconds of everything. You look starved. Want some orange juice? How about a little strawberry jam on your toast?"

AN HOUR LATER, at six-thirty, Larinda hurried out with Cash to open the gate. Sellers were already lined up bumper-to-bumper in cars and trucks.

There were two lanes of vehicles, Cash pointed out, one for the monthly reserved spaces and one for day spaces on a first-come, first-served, cash basis. Each market space was numbered on a map. He would assign spaces; she would cashier. He explained that the main gate for shoppers opened at eight-thirty. The day cashier would collect the nominal fee charged for shopper parking.

"My main concern today," Cash said as he unlocked the drive-up window, "is whether it's going to rain or not. The weather report says no, but I'm not convinced." He surveyed the clouds that were gathering in the sky. "If it does, we'll be busy issuing rain checks. The cutoff time for them is at 11:00 a.m. Nothing is worse for a flea-market's profit than rain."

Larinda nodded and stepped into the check-in kiosk with him. She knew rain. Gigantic sheets of it, and gale-force winds, could destroy years of hard work in a matter of minutes. Who knew it better than she?

But there was no time to dwell on what she had lost. The first vendor in line drove up at Cash's signal and handed her his space fee.

"These people are going to get spoiled," Cash whispered to her after several vendors had passed into the market. "When I do this alone, it takes twice as long."

"Everyone's so friendly I can't imagine them honking their horns for you to hurry," she said.

"Talk about friendly, here's one of the friendliest you'll ever meet." Cash winked at the next driver, a tiny, wizened woman. "Hi, Mrs. Soames. Back with more toaster covers?"

"A trunkful, you good-looking devil," Mrs. Soames replied with a grin that showed more gums than teeth. "My crochet hook has been breaking the speed limit. Who's your pretty girlfriend?"

"You mean my pretty landlady," Cash corrected. "This is Larinda. She just got lucky and inherited the Moonglow."

Smiling, Mrs. Soames studied her. "Pleased to meet you, dear. May I put a suggestion in your suggestion box?"

"Of course. What is it?"

"Bring back the movies. The Moonglow is the only drive-in this area has ever had. Folks miss it. *I* miss it. I used to come here with my third husband before I married him. Herbert, Lord keep him, was almost as handsome as Cash here. I can tell you I didn't come with him just to watch the movies."

Cash laughed out loud.

Mrs. Soames beamed. "That's one of the best things about a drive-in, isn't it? I tell you I hate to think that young folk around here will grow up and go to their graves without the Moonglow for entertainment. It's a chunk of American movie history. Bring it back, Larinda."

"I'll give it some thought."

"I know you will." With a final wink at Cash, Mrs. Soames drove on.

Cash gave Larinda a wary, sidelong glance. "You aren't really going to give it some thought, are you?"

"Of course not. I was just being polite to my elders."

"Good. Movies are one headache I don't need. Closing earlier, rushing to clean up, lower concession profits—no, thanks." He lapsed back into his devilish grin and muttered, "My girlfriend, eh? What made her think that?"

Larinda raised an eyebrow at him. "Her bifocals. She was looking through the wrong half."

"What do you think, Fred?" Cash asked the next driver, whose T-shirt proclaimed him a honey farmer. "Was Mrs. Soames seeing wrong when she mistook this pretty lady for my girlfriend?"

Fred shook his head. "Not Mrs. Soames. That woman has second sight. If she took you for his girlfriend, you'll be his girlfriend—if you aren't already."

"Am not, never was and don't intend to be," Larinda declared. "All I'm doing here is lending a helping hand for the day."

Fred shook his head. "That's what *you* think. Mrs. Soames *knows*."

"Cash, tell him," Larinda appealed.

"Tell him what?"

"That there's nothing between us."

Cash's eyes teased. "Nothing? After I tucked you into bed last night?"

"Don't believe a thing he says," Larinda advised the farmer. She took his money and rapidly made change.

Mischief in his smile, Cash persevered. "After I popped a bottle of champagne in the wee hours just for you?"

"I am *not* his girlfriend," she emphasized to Fred. "The champagne was—"

"After champagne and roses and breakfast together at dawn this morning, Larinda? After all that, you want me to lie about us?"

"Pardon, ma'am," Fred said, returning a ten-dollar bill from the change she had given him, "you only owe me five back."

She replaced the ten with a five and flashed Cash a sharp look. "There is absolutely, positively zero truth to anything he's said."

Fred nodded, his eyes rife with speculation. "I can see that without listening, ma'am." Still nodding, he drove through.

As the next vehicle came forward, Larinda directed a dark scowl at Cash. "Keep teasing like this and you'll lose money."

"What if I do?"

"I won't be held responsible for the loss, that's what." She handled the next fee and made change—correct change—despite Cash's amused attention to her every move.

"Much better," he said approvingly.

"Only because you kept your mouth shut, Cash."

He couldn't resist. "I don't when I kiss, Larinda. Do *you?*"

"I am not his girlfriend," she emphasized to Fred.

4

LARINDA LET Cash's provocative question hang unanswered in the air between them. If French kisses were his preference, she was in trouble. Because they were hers, as well.

"Just kidding," Cash said when the air grew too thick to breathe. He was glad Larinda was looking everywhere but at him. She'd see a man who wanted to kiss her. She'd see him looking pretty damned red faced at what he'd so recklessly blurted out. Flirting. What was wrong with him? He'd better shut up.

He did. She, too, remained silent. They worked together like that until the last seller paid and drove through.

She handed Cash the money drawer. "What else can I do to pay my way until the van is fixed?"

"Ask me after you get back from Western Union." He gave her his car keys and told her how to get there. "My car's in the carport behind my trailer. She's a beaut. Be careful with her."

Cash watched Larinda walk away. What was it about this woman that made it so easy for him to pass over the keys to his cherished car? She moved with the purposeful stride of a woman who had a full schedule of places to go, things to do. Nothing in her step hinted that she had no choice but to return to Anaheim and the deli—or live in her trailer at the Moonglow and work in Weston for a year.

He knew how it felt to have no place to go. He'd cashed his last unemployment check, when Chester had contacted him out of the blue. Without Chester, he'd have become one more timber-town unemployment statistic like the loggers he'd left behind in Oregon. He couldn't help identifying with Larinda's predicament, or admiring the way she could still square her shoulders after losing out to a hurricane and a surprise lease amendment.

He watched her hair swing side to side where it spilled down her back. It was long enough to cover her breasts in front and make him want to comb his fingers through its glossy abundance of waves and curls. Long enough and red enough to make him want it flaming all over him and scorching his skin.

Larinda sensed that Cash was watching her as she walked away. She was sure he was sexually appraising her. She was just as certain that he was worried she'd put a dent in his "beaut" of a car before she got back from Western Union. Men never referred to automobiles as "she" if they weren't hopelessly in love with them.

She saw why with her first glimpse of the car. It was that irresistible classic of classics, a two-door, candy-apple red '57 Chevy convertible. Larinda felt sixteen again as she drove it out of the Moonglow and into Weston. She found a Golden Oldies radio station and sang "Love Me Tender" along with Elvis. Wasn't *Love Me Tender* his movie debut? Yes. His singing was the highlight of the film.

During the song she glanced at the passenger seat. If she hadn't fallen asleep last night, she'd have ridden there beside Cash to a nice dinner. After dinner in Weston she'd have ridden back next to him.

She mused that if the radio had played fifties love songs, Cash might well have slid his right arm along the back of her seat and pulled her close. He might even have tried to kiss her. With a man like him in a car like this, she might have let him.

She shivered, wishing she could defuse the sexual awareness she'd felt from the first moment she'd seen Cash. It helped to think about the restrictive terms of Jethro's will and Cash's lease amendment. She shook off any lingering feelings of attraction. Damn Cash and his stubborn resistance to selling out! He stood in the way of everything she wanted.

She could almost taste the video store she could have if he'd only sell out to her. With him refusing top price for his lease, she owned a non-liquid asset that generated only enough income to pay its taxes and keep small change in her pocket. That wasn't enough for her to feel safe and secure.

She fumed as she pulled up to the wire service office to collect her father's loan, *now I'm even more in debt. And I can't pay any of it off until my insurance pays up.*

The clerk was a portly, grandfatherly gentleman with hazel eyes that twinkled at her in welcome. His name tag said "Roy."

"I'll bet you're Larinda Outlaw come for the money your dad wired in this morning," he said.

Larinda stared at him in surprise. "How do you know who I am?"

"Easy. Walt Whitman's an old pal of mine. He stopped by and filled me in on his way home this morning." Handing her some paperwork to sign, he added, "Too bad you're not going to fix up the old passion pit for movies. It was a heck of a place in its glory days."

"Whoever buys it from me will have to do the fixing up," she told him. "I'm planning to sell as soon—" she thought of Cash, her nemesis "—as soon as the current leaseholder sells me his lease."

"I hear he's not anxious," said Roy. "Maybe while you're waiting him out, you can talk to a few of the land developers around town. I heard one of the biggest was sniffing around out Moonglow way not long ago. Davis Development, I believe it was. Suburbs around here are eating up farmland right and left lately."

Larinda thought of the restrictive stipulation in Jethro's will, forbidding any negotiation of a sale until the leasehold expired. She slid the signed paperwork back to Roy.

"Davis Development," she repeated, more out of courtesy than true interest. "I'll keep it in mind." If not for the quirk in the will, she'd be on the developer's doorstep in two minutes.

His expression a bit mournful, Roy counted out her money. "No chance of movies by night, flea market by day? You're sure about that?"

"Quite sure." He sounded as nostalgic for the good old glory days as Mrs. Soames had sounded early this morning, Larinda thought. It made her momentarily wonder how many other Westonians were still mourning the demise of the drive-in.

Watching her fold the cash into her wallet, Roy advised, "You'd better take that to the bank next door and put it into traveler's checks to be safe."

"Just what I was thinking, Roy. Thanks so much."

Waving goodbye, Larinda left and walked the few steps to the bank. The teller there, a young woman who was name-tagged "Jennifer," had a big smile for her.

"The safest traveler's checks you have, please," Larinda requested, laying out her money.

"You must be Larinda Outlaw," Jennifer said.

Larinda blinked. "First Roy at the wire service, now you. What is this, a Weston conspiracy? Or does Walt Whitman swing by here, too, on his way home from work?"

"No, his wife and my mom are friends. Word gets around in a small place . . . and your hair *is* the reddest in town." Though busily preparing Larinda's checks for her to sign, Jennifer seemed to have something else on her mind. "It sure would be neat if you'd make the Moonglow a drive-in again."

Feeling like a broken record, Larinda told Jennifer what she'd told Roy. The teller let out a sigh. As a movie lover herself, Larinda could sympathize. But resurrecting her inheritance wasn't in her plan. Perhaps word of that would get around as quickly as word of her arrival.

Larinda left the bank with her checks and drove back to the Moonglow. Seeing Cash's relieved expression when she entered his office, she knew he'd been worrying about the Chevy's welfare.

"What's this I hear in town about Davis Development sniffing out land to develop in this area?" she asked, returning his keys to him.

He shrugged. "Vague rumors have a way of becoming facts overnight in small towns. I don't pay much attention." He jingled the keys in his hand. "Any trouble with the car?"

"No nicks, no dents, no scrapes," she assured him. "She's still a beaut. Many thanks."

"They rightfully go to my father," Cash said. "She's mine through him."

Like the lease, Larinda thought resentfully. But Cash's grim expression reminded her of the loss he'd suffered. Feeling a rush of sympathy, she reached across the scarred surface of the desk and touched Cash's hand. "I'm sorry he's gone."

Cash curled his fingers around hers, then met her gaze. "Me, too . . . even though I hardly knew him."

"Oh. I didn't—"

"Dad!" Dan exclaimed, rushing through the open door with his duffel bag. He stopped short, his mouth open. "Whatcha doin' holdin' hands?"

"Nothing," Cash said, breaking the contact. "What are *you* doing back so early from Jeffie's?"

"He got sick after breakfast." Dan's eyes widened. "It was gross. He barfed up pancakes all over the—"

"We get the picture," Cash cut in, darting an apologetic glance at Larinda before returning his attention to his son. "Where's Melanie?"

"Right here," a shapely young woman said, stepping through the doorway. "Hi, Cash."

Her black hair and green eyes made Larinda think Melanie had been named for the wrong character in *Gone With the Wind*.

"Jeffie's caught the flu bug, it seems," Melanie said.

"Yeah," Dan agreed. "A giant flu bug."

Melanie tousled the boy's hair. "Let's hope it didn't catch *you*, Danny boy." To Cash, she said, "I figured the quicker I hustled him away, the less chance he'd catch what Jeffie's got."

Larinda saw her look at Cash the way Scarlett O'Hara had looked at Rhett Butler. What with Fran and Eva, and Melanie today, Larinda doubted that any woman in Weston would kick Cash Bowman out of bed. Yet according to Fran, he slept alone.

"Before you go," Cash said, "meet Larinda Outlaw, my landlady. Larinda, meet Melanie Potts, Jeffie's mother."

Jeffie's divorced *mother?* Larinda silently speculated, exchanging a nod of greeting with the woman.

Melanie backed toward the door. "I've got to get. Hubby's a good man on a hay baler, but not much of a nurse." A quick wave and she was gone.

Hubby. Larinda was feeling the oddest sense of relief when Dan asked her, "Did you sleep in the bed we made for you?"

"Yes, I did, Dan. I didn't know you helped make it. Thank you." She looked at Cash. "Both of you."

"You're welcome," Cash said in unison with Dan. He rose from behind the desk. "Let's get you unpacked, Scout."

Larinda rose, too. "How else can I help around here, Cash?"

"Well . . ." He rubbed the back of his neck. "*I'd* have time to make a market check for stolen goods if *you* could set Dan to rights for me."

"I'd love to. Anything else?"

"Help me clean my room," Dan piped up. "It's a disaster area."

Cash raised his eyebrows and looked hopeful. "Would you mind?"

"Not at all. I have tonight's dinner to earn and breakfast tomorrow, too. Remember?"

Dan jumped up and down. "Dinner with *us*? Yippee! Can we go out to Burger Baron, Dad?"

"Yep." He looked at Larinda. "Burgers, onion rings, root-beer floats. They're not candlelight and wine, but Dan's not into the fancy stuff."

"Burgers are fine," Larinda said.

Dan chattered away about his night at Jeffie's as he led Larinda to the trailer.

Feeling abandoned, Cash wandered out after them and watched them go. He saw his son's little hand curl into Larinda's and hang on tight. Cash turned away from the sight of Dan's eager smile. The boy craved a mother. One mother-hungry boy. One redhead-hungry man. Good thing she didn't want to stick around beyond tomorrow.

Cash looked up at the cloudy sky, and thought about what a godsend it would be if it rained only on the days the market was closed. He needed every dry Saturday, Sunday, Tuesday and Thursday that Mother Nature could spare for the next twelve months. Larinda would have the Moonglow up for sale the instant the lease expired. Good thing she was leaving, he reiterated to himself. Out of sight, out of mind.

He lowered his gaze to the mass of market goers and noticed a large crowd forming where the two Purvis rug stands stood. Otis and Otto, at it again.

Cash gritted his teeth and rolled up his sleeves. Thank God for the Purvis brothers today. A man couldn't ask for anything better to take his mind off wanting Larinda.

FOR THE BETTER PART of an hour he was too steamed at Otis and Otto to think of Larinda even once. As soon as he cooled down, though, he started thinking too much of her. He couldn't shake that vivid image of her spread out on her bed last night. He began prowling through the market, always on the watch for her. It wouldn't take her all day to help Dan clean his room.

Finally, right around noon, he spotted her over at a bent-willow furniture stand. Dan was at her side and the two of them were inspecting not the lawn furniture but the rusty speaker post next to the stand.

Cash strode through the crowd, wishing that Mrs. Soames had never urged Larinda to show movies. Larinda appeared to be getting ideas he didn't want in her head.

"What's up?" he asked when he reached them. "Is your room clean, Dan?"

Dan nodded. "Can I go wash carrots at the vegetable stand?"

"Sure. Go."

Cash turned to Larinda as Dan ran off. He kicked the speaker post, gratified to see rust flakes rain down from it. "They're all in bad shape."

"So I see," she said.

Openly eavesdropping, the bent-willow vendor said, "Not such bad shape. Straighten 'em out, scour the rust off, they'll work just fine."

Larinda raised her eyebrows. "Really?"

The vendor, a retiree in a sweat suit, tipped his baseball cap. "I had a metal-pipe business before I retired."

"She doesn't need any repair estimates," Cash said, taking Larinda's elbow to steer her firmly away. "She's leaving tomorrow."

Larinda had never liked being manhandled. She didn't like it now. A few steps away from the bent-willow display, she pulled her elbow from Cash's grasp.

"I could have told him that myself," she said.

He just smiled. "I saved you the trouble. Get that guy started talking metal pipe and bent-willow lawn chairs and he never shuts up. One of those."

"Oh." Larinda glanced over her shoulder at the man. "He didn't *look* that talkative."

"Well, he is. I know. What are you up to now that Dan's room is shipshape?"

"Nothing. I thought I'd wander around and see what the market is all about."

She looked up at him, her heart beating a little faster. His eyes were enough to make any woman's heart do aerobics. Feeling a lingering warmth where his hand had grasped her elbow, she wondered how his French kisses might feel on her lips.

Abruptly, she looked down and took a step back from him. How silly to be mooning over him as if he were a matinee idol.

"What are *you* up to?" she asked.

Up to no good, he thought, fighting a desire to take a taste of his landlady's lush lips. It didn't seem to matter that she wanted to put him out of business. He was conscious only of a flare of desire.

"I'm . . . always checking for stolen goods," he replied, backing away. "So far, so good. See you later."

Larinda gave a little wave and moved off in the opposite direction. She suppressed the urge to fan her face with both hands to cool the heat she felt curling through her. As she walked through the market, she searched for Dan. Finding him at a vegetable stand, she stopped in the shade of its awning for a rest.

Dan introduced her to Annie, the produce vendor, before running off to play with a friend. Annie was young and sturdy, an earth-mother type. Tying the carrots Dan had washed into bunches, she gave Larinda a friendly smile.

"Mrs. Soames was telling me earlier that you've inherited this place. What are your plans for it?"

"I haven't decided yet," Larinda hedged. She didn't want to go into the lease complications and Cash's obstinacy. "I'm going back home to Anaheim tomorrow to think about it."

"You're now the envy of every single woman in Weston, you know," Annie said. "They'd all give their eye-teeth to be Cash's landlady. More than his landlady, if you catch my drift."

Larinda nodded. "He's awfully good-looking," she allowed. "Are you one of the singles who'd spare an eyetooth?"

"I might if I wasn't crazy about my husband and kids," Annie said, grinning.

A moment later, Cash emerged from the crowd, and stopped when he saw Larinda.

"Speak of the handsome devil," Annie murmured.

"Hi, ladies," One glance at their flushed faces told Cash they'd been gossiping—about him. It made him feel acutely self-conscious. He never felt this uncomfortable when it was just Weston women speculating about his love life.

He was glad when one of the market shoppers stopped to ask him several questions. He turned his back to the vegetable stand. Annie turned to serve a customer.

Though unobserved, Larinda tried not to direct too many lingering glances at Cash. He was more than good-looking. He was superb—in both looks and build. The singles hotline must have been buzzing ever since he'd hit town. The hotline in Oregon had probably been disconnected the day he left.

Cash turned from the inquiring shopper and caught Larinda staring. "What?" he said to her as the shopper walked away.

"Uh . . . just wondering if you'd prefer that I cook dinner tonight, rather than going to Burger Baron."

"No need. Dan's looking forward to the Baron. That all right with you and your rain check?"

"Fine." But she'd much rather cook than be taken out to dinner. A homey evening would be nice. She stopped the thought, uncomfortable with the domestic cravings she'd been having ever since the hurricane. A burger joint would be great, just great.

BURGER BARON turned out to be quick and enjoyable. Larinda experienced no domestic urges during her fast-food dinner. She and Cash shared light conversation. Dan's chatter filled in the gaps.

Returning to the Moonglow with Cash and Dan, she accepted Cash's invitation to his trailer for a cup of coffee.

Dan disappeared into his room to watch a Charlie Brown special on TV. Larinda sat at the kitchen table and watched Cash make coffee.

She had no trouble imagining him in a plaid work-shirt and yellow hard-hat, felling Oregon timber up north. The way his muscles flexed under his form-fitting cotton T-shirt right now, he could have been stacking cordwood rather than measuring coffee grounds into a paper filter.

She contemplated the back pockets of his slim-hipped jeans and wondered, when he made love, if he called out "Timmmberrr" at the moment of truth.

Cash turned and caught her looking at him just as he had earlier.

"What?" he said.

She had to come up with a quick response. "Uh, d'you think Dan would mind me watching Charlie Brown with him until the coffee's done?"

"Mind? Is the Pope Protestant?"

"I'll do that, then." She left the table and disappeared into Dan's room.

Scowling, Cash dried his hands. He didn't like it that she'd checked out the fit of his jeans and preferred a kid's show to his company. He threw the towel aside. He didn't like anything he'd been thinking or feeling since she'd shown up. He also didn't like having nothing to do but watch coffee drip into a glass pot.

He went to the broom closet and pulled out a box that held some of Chester's old things. He hadn't sorted through it yet. Now was a good time to start.

Cash set the box on the kitchen table and began emptying it of paperback books, pencils, erasers, notepads and old tax returns. Halfway down the box he came to a jumble of check stubs, bank statements and correspondence. Some of the statements hadn't been opened.

Two envelopes, also unopened, were from a Hollywood legal firm. The letters Larinda had mentioned yesterday? Cash broke the seals and read the contents. Yes, they were first and second notifications of Jethro's death and Larinda's inheritance.

It didn't surprise him that the letters, bank statements and bills had been stashed away unopened. In his one month with Chester before the auto accident, he had learned that his father's attitude toward business had been very casual. Chester's procrastinating had almost prevented him from contacting Cash before it was too late.

At the bottom of the box, Cash found a photo album with snapshots of his mother, Verna. There were others of Verna and Chester together. He sat back and studied the pictures of his mother and father. Just before the accident, Chester had told him about their short, bitter marriage and how it had ended six months after Cash was born.

Verna had considered the subject closed for as long as Cash could remember. After her divorce from Chester, she had put a permanent lock on that unhappy segment of her life. "He didn't want kids period. *I* did" was all she had ever replied to Cash's natural questions about his father.

Cash's stepfather had been the only father he'd known. A *good* stepfather. Dads didn't come any better than Raymond Johnson. He'd treated Cash no differently from the two sons he'd fathered with Verna. Cash loved Ray and his stepbrothers and always would.

"It's true I never wanted kids," Chester had told him. "Never had a happy childhood myself, so I didn't trust myself to give one to you. Doesn't mean I didn't think of you, though. I did. Never had enough money or I'd have sent it for your keep. Always wondered what you looked like. Didn't want to die without finding out."

Chester had sighed, tears in his blue-flecked gray eyes. "Age does things to a man. Makes him look back in regret. Makes him pick up the phone and hope his own flesh and blood will forgive him."

Remembering his father's tears, Cash cleared his throat. He switched his focus to Verna's face in the photograph, recalling how furious she had been when he'd told her that Chester had not only contacted him but invited him down to run the flea market with him.

"Flea market!" she had sneered. "Just where I'd expect a drifter like him to end up. What has he ever done for you? Nothing."

"He sounded sorry on the phone, Mom."

"Cash, sorry is what you'll be if you go down there."

"He's offering me a job and decent pay. God knows I need both with logging shut down here. And Dan might as well meet his blood grandfather."

Cash knew now that he'd done the right thing in going against Verna's advice and overriding her objections. He hadn't regretted it. He'd only been sorry that Chester hadn't made that phone call earlier. Cash had liked what little he'd known of his father. So had Dan.

"Cash?"

He looked up and saw Larinda standing across the table from him.

"Dan's nodding off," she said. "Another few minutes of the Peanuts gang and he'll be gone. If you're busy, I can get him ready for bed."

He closed the album. "I'll do it. None of this stuff is crucial."

"What *is* this stuff?"

"Things I haven't gone through since my father died. The letters from the law firm are there. He hadn't opened them." He stood and headed for Dan's room. "Finish emptying the box, if you like," he said over his shoulder. "I'll be back in a sec."

After pouring herself a cup of coffee, Larinda reached into the box and drew out a square, lettered wall plaque. "Happiness," it read, "isn't having what you want. It's wanting what you have."

She propped it up against the box and dipped back in for a scant handful of envelopes that appeared to contain letters. They were addressed to Chester from Jethro Everly. She arranged them in chronological order by postmark, then sat sipping her coffee.

She had been curious about Jethro all her life and was interested to know what he'd written to Chester. All the attorney had said was that the two men were friends from way back. When had they met? How had they become friends?

"'Night, Scout," she heard Cash say from the door of Dan's room. "Sleep tight."

Cash joined her at the table. He picked up the plaque. "What's this?"

"Your father's philosophy of life, I'd guess."

Cash nodded. "He had a habit of saying that."

"If it's true," Larinda said, "I should be content with leasing you the Moonglow instead of wanting to buy the video store. Hah."

"If you were," said Cash, "I could get the business degree I want in the two years I need to get it."

Careful not to raise her voice and wake Dan, Larinda retorted in an undertone, "What you have is my very generous offer to buy your lease."

"Your offer doesn't come close to the income I can get out of this place the next twelve months."

"In other words, you're not sold on Chester's philosophy?"

Cash flipped the plaque facedown on the table. "No sale. What else did you dig up?"

Frustrated and peeved, Larinda pushed back from the table. "Nothing I feel like poring over with an arch enemy."

"Fine with me."

"Me, too."

LARINDA HAD NOTHING ELSE to do but stew all alone in her trailer. No TV. No radio. No book. No magazine.

She paced through her tiny kitchen, her little living room, her short hallway. The bedroom was no good for pacing. It was too full of bed. She thought of Cash in his cozy, fully furnished trailer choosing among many things to do. Watch TV...read a book or magazine...flex his gorgeous muscles under his T-shirt....

What she wouldn't give for a good video right now, a sexy drama starring Dennis Quaid or Kevin Costner or Harrison Ford. Any one of those three hunks would take her mind off the infuriating man next door in no time at all. Without them, she was stuck with Cash at the epicenter of every thought.

She stopped, mid-pace, in the kitchen. Why do this inside when she could do it outside and really let off some steam? A look out the window made her think twice about a brisk walk around the grounds. It looked breezy out there, and cloudy, as well—almost as if it might rain.

Breathing deeply, she told herself she couldn't let every little possibility of wind and rain keep her inside. At some point, someday, it was going to rain and blow and she was going to have to confront her fears. This wasn't hurricane country. It was California. After years of drought in this state, rain should be considered a godsend rather than a natural disaster.

Determined to be brave, she left the trailer and walked a full circuit around the drive-in. In the middle of a second trip, she met up with the night watchman.

"'Evening, Larinda," Walt said after shining his heavy-duty flashlight at her.

"Hi, Walt." The clouds and breeze seemed less fearsome to her with Walt and his bright light present. "What are you up to?"

"Making sure no one's here who shouldn't be. What about you?"

She shrugged, trying not to appear apprehensive about the weather. "Just out for a breath of fresh air and a look around."

"It's a pity about this place, isn't it?" he said, gazing up toward the dark hulk of the movie screen. "My wife and I used to bring our kids here to the show. Now there's no show for them to bring *their* kids to."

Larinda nodded. "Yes, it's too bad."

"No chance you'd consider fixing it up and running movies again, I suppose?"

"No chance, Walt," she said for the fourth time that day.

"First-runs would probably cost too much, I grant you," he mused. "But old movies might make a decent

profit, double features and the like. With indoor theater prices sky-high these days, folks here wouldn't need
much excuse to pack this place if the price was right."
He winked. "Specially the high-school and college
crowd. Hormones at that age do love a drive-in."

After wishing Larinda a pleasant good-night, Walt
moved on. She watched his flashlight bob out of sight
around the concession building. *Old movies.* She stared
up at the night sky and the outline of the screen. Above
it a misty slice of moon peeked through the clouds.
Double features.

Fixing the place up could be possible. Walt was right
about first-runs being too expensive. But handpicked
vintage double features paired to draw a wide range of
viewers just might pack them in. Theoretically, of
course.

Recalling that the movie projector was still in excel-
lent condition, Larinda felt a thrilling jolt travel up her
spine. She forced it back down. A video store was what
she wanted, she reminded herself, not a has-been drive-
in. Repairing the Moonglow would use up too much of
her insurance money.

She headed back to the trailer. Her wayward mind
speculated that if she fixed up the Moonglow she'd be
running her own business until she could sell the place
in a year. As a thriving drive-in, its worth might enable
her to open two video stores instead of—

A large raindrop hit her cheek and the sound of rising wind echoed in her ear. Her heart and mind
stopped. Another drop landed, then another. Her rib
cage contracted. She froze in mid-step. *Rain...wind...*

Images from the hurricane rushed up, flooding her
with panic. She'd seen roofs torn from office build-

ings. Loaded trucks had tumbled end over end in gale-force winds. A neighborhood of brick houses had been washed away.

Run! She wheeled around. A swoosh of stiff breeze lifted her hair away from her shoulders and back. Another drop of rain slashed her face. *Run!* It was all she could think, all she could do.

She cringed from fitful gusts of wind as she raced toward her trailer. *Faster. Faster.* Terrified, unseeing, she plowed into Cash a few yards from the two trailers.

"Whoa, there," he said, steadying her by the shoulders. "Try watching where you're headed next time."

"Cash . . ." She rocked back in his grip.

He felt her tremble, then start to shake violently. "Red? What's wrong?"

"Rain . . . it—scares me."

"Rain? Why?"

"Because of the h-h-hur—"

In a flash he understood. Hurricane. He'd never experienced one, but he'd battled raging forest fires and witnessed the destruction they'd wrought. He'd seen terror-stricken deer fleeing in droves. Larinda had the same look. She had lived through a hurricane, but she apparently hadn't weathered it.

"It's just a drop or two," he soothed, curving an arm around her protectively.

She burrowed against his chest and clung to him. "Hold me," she whimpered. "Help m-me."

He gathered her into his arms, stroked her hair, whispered that nothing could hurt her. "This isn't Texas," he reassured. "You're safe from hurricanes here." Rocking her gently, he held her tight. "The wind's dying down."

Larinda expelled a shaky sigh. Slowly, hesitantly, she straightened in the warmth of his embrace.

"Thank you, Cash."

"No problem." He paused, then asked," You've been this way since Texas?"

She nodded. "They call it posttraumatic stress disorder. I'm sorry I—"

He silenced her with a press of his fingers against her spine. "Don't be. I know forest fire survivors who can't strike a match without falling apart. It passes with time, they say."

"There's hope for me? That's good news." She managed an unsteady laugh, although her knees still shook. She braced her hands at his waist to balance herself.

"Hold on," he invited. "Catch up with yourself."

She laid her cheek to his chest. It took several minutes for her to calm down and in that space of time Cash's arms tightened around her. His heart sounded against her ear. Against her middle, through her cotton sweater, she felt the press of his belt buckle. His fingers moved up through her hair then molded to the curve of her head.

Larinda angled her face up to look at him. His fingers pressed against her scalp and drew her head closer. Her knees shook, but for a different reason now.

Cash recognized the difference in the rise of her breasts against him, the parting of her lips. He thought, for just an instant, that kissing her would be the biggest mistake he could make.

The next instant, he whispered, "Remember what I said when you told me to keep my mouth shut this morning?"

"Yes," she murmured back. "You said you don't when you kiss."

"I meant it, Red." He slid his lower lip between hers and grazed it along the edges of her front teeth. Then, quite simply, he took her mouth. She returned his kiss with the same intensity. The silent, stroking dialogue of their tongues became both argument and acquiescence, conflict and communion, duel and delight.

Cash wound his fingers in her hair to better hold her warm, responsive mouth to his. He felt the way her lips followed his, invited more of his kiss. He drew her further into it, into a slow, deep, seductive taste.

Seduced, Larinda slid her hands into his back pockets to better hold his hard, yearning hips to hers. She arched her throat toward him and surrendered the depth, the intimate flavors and textures he was seeking.

She wanted it to end. She wanted it to last. She wanted to break free of him, yet longed to stay. No. She couldn't stay, couldn't want more, couldn't get involved. No. Heartbreak number three wasn't in her plans.

Feeling her tense, Cash lifted his mouth from hers. "Don't say you didn't want this," he murmured. "You did. And you do."

"So did you," she shakily countered.

"You don't make life easy for a man, Red."

She was glad he'd said that. It gave her a strong enough reason to pull away from him. It refreshed her memory of why getting involved with men—with Cash—could only lead to minor tragedy of one kind or another. If she wanted heartbreak, she could always get it in a movie like *Wuthering Heights*.

"My name is Larinda. Get that straight." She pushed past him and stepped toward her trailer. "Good night."

"Just for the record," he said casually as he turned toward his door, "my favorite color has always been red."

5

THE NEXT MORNING, Larinda awoke to a knock on her door. She hurried into her clothes.

"You've got a phone call at our house," Dan said when she opened the door. "The guy says it's urgent."

When she rushed into the trailer with Dan, Cash didn't look up from buttering toast at the table. That was a plus, she thought, still rubbing sleep from her eyes. It was an added plus that the phone was across the room from him. In contrast to her disheveled state, he was freshly showered and shaved.

She picked up the receiver. "Hello?"

"Hey, there, this is Lonnie at the garage. Your van's going to take longer than I thought."

"How much longer?"

"Another day. I've got a mechanic out sick. Flu bug."

"One more day?" She stifled a groan. "You're sure?"

"When flu's going around, I take it one day at a time. Know what I mean?"

Larinda knew. "I'll be there this time tomorrow morning to pick it up," she told him, hoping the threat would make the van first priority.

"Better call first," he said.

Larinda hung up and raked her fingers through her sleep-tangled hair. "Damn."

Cash looked up. "Coffee? Black?"

"Yes, thank you. After I get human."

"You look okay." His tone was carefully neutral as he poured her a cup. "Dan and I have a few minutes before we leave."

She moved to the table and curled her fingers around the cup, unsure of what to say or how to act. She still felt a lingering sense of surprise over the tenderness Cash had shown the night before. She didn't know what to make of it—or the kiss that had followed it. It seemed best to proceed as if it had all happened too long ago to remember.

"You have school today?" she asked, breaking the thick silence between them.

He nodded. "Monday, Wednesday, Friday. Same hours as Dan. Works out great, since the market's closed those days and open the the rest of the week."

"When do you get a day off?"

"Whenever a holiday rolls around, I guess. Dan and school and homework and the market keep me running otherwise." He glanced at the box he'd pushed aside from the night before. "That's why I haven't sorted through this stuff." He paused for a swallow of his coffee. "Those letters from Jethro to my father are interesting. They met while they were stationed together during the war."

"Which war?"

"Korean. Jethro saved him from a sniper's bullet. That's apparently why he ended up being my godfather years later. I didn't know that, though, until a month ago. How'd he get to be yours, too?"

Larinda explained her parents' link to Jethro. "How is it," she then asked, "that you didn't know Chester until recently?"

Over a second cup of coffee, Cash told her about Verna and Chester and Raymond Johnson. "So here I am," he concluded, "somewhere I never thought I'd be."

"Me, too," Larinda said with a sigh. "Stuck here for another day with nothing to do. If the market were open, I could at least work."

Cash shrugged. "If you drop me off at school, you can have the car for the day. Drive around. See the sights. Weston's not a metropolis, but it's not dullsville, either. The downtown mall has some charm. More than the timber town I left in Oregon."

She kept her eyes on her cup. "The longer I have to stay, the more I owe you."

"Maybe you'd like to even it out by cooking dinner," he suggested. "I'll take you up on the offer you made yesterday."

Larinda nodded gratefully.

SO LARINDA DROPPED Dan and Cash off and spent the day exploring Weston. Cash had been right about the midtown pedestrian mall's charm. It had old-fashioned streetlamps, rows of trees, comfortable benches and an outdoor café or two. The civic-center plaza and buildings were new.

She wandered from city hall into the public library, where she browsed through books, magazines and finally the video section. Studying the titles available, she spotted *Wild West*. She smiled, thinking of the scene her parents were in.

Old movies. Double features. She recalled her conversation with Walt. The idea of refurbishing the drive-in had been trying to root in her head for two days and

Walt had fertilized it last night. But it wasn't what she—
or Cash—wanted, she reminded herself. She didn't
know the first thing about operating a drive-in theater.
She didn't even know if it was feasible in this day and
age. Did it make sense to consider the possibility? What
was the profit-loss margin for a drive-in these days?

Ten minutes later, aided by newspaper and magazine articles on microfilm, she was answering her own
questions. Recent articles informed her that fifteen
hundred drive-ins remained nationwide, down from a
heyday high of more than five thousand in the late
fifties. Now an endangered species of Americana,
drive-ins flourished only in certain areas.

The people of Asheville, Tennessee, had success-
fully lobbied to bring their local theater back from being only a flea market. She read that a six-screen theater
in the San Francisco Bay area regularly packed in five
to six thousand viewers every weekend. It seemed that
the right theater in the right place could not only survive, but prosper.

Was the Moonglow the right theater? Was Weston the
right place? Were Mrs. Soames and Walt Whitman onto
something?

"No," Larinda said under her breath. She switched
the microfilm screen off. Every word of what she had
read, however, whispered yes to her.

Weighing every pro and con she could conceive of,
every risk and uncertainty, Larinda left the library to
pick Dan and Cash up from school. Dan was full of
classroom chatter all the way to the college, where Cash
waited at the main corner with several other students.
He was handing a book to one of them, an attractive
coed, when Larinda and Dan drove up.

"Thanks for loaning it to me," Larinda heard him say through the car window.

"Anytime, Cash."

Larinda heard a purr in the young woman's tone, and saw in her blue eyes the same look she'd seen in Melanie's yesterday. If Cash slept alone, it was obviously by choice. She remembered his hungry kiss. Why, with every woman in Weston lusting after him, was he hungry for her?

Larinda stopped the car and Dan climbed into the back seat. She slid to the passenger half of the front seat so Cash could drive. Glancing out the side window, she caught the full force of an envious blue stare.

It only stood to reason, she told herself as Cash steered the Chevy away from the curb. He had the sexy good looks, rugged build and confident attitude women liked. He had a charming little boy who needed mothering. No woman's deepest female instincts were safe where he and Dan were concerned.

She too couldn't keep her eyes off Cash. Even now she had difficulty looking straight ahead instead of straight at him. Nor had she been able to keep herself from mothering Dan. So it was no wonder that Weston women had eyes for the Bowman boys.

"Dad, can we go bowling tonight?" Dan asked from the back seat.

Cash looked over at Larinda. "Feel like it?"

"I can't afford to owe you for that, also," she said, shaking her head.

"We'll owe *you*," he persisted, "if you cook dinner beforehand."

"Yeah," Dan put in. "What's for dinner, Larinda?"

Cash raised an eyebrow. "Tuna casserole, maybe? There's everything you need for it at home."

"Yum," said Dan. "My favorite."

Larinda kept shaking her head. "That's hardly a fair trade. Why don't I just keep score at the bowling alley?"

"The way I cook, it's more than fair," Cash said. "Dan's sick of soup-and-sandwich dinners…and so am I. *You* cook dinner. *We'll take you bowling.*"

Larinda couldn't let it pass that easily. "It wouldn't really be fair unless I baked cookies for dessert."

"Yum!" the two Bowmans agreed in unison. Cash pushed the speed limit all the way home.

After baking three dozen oatmeal chewies in Cash's compact kitchen, Larinda turned to layering tuna and noodles in a casserole dish. Cash and Dan did their homework together at the table and drooled over the cookies she wouldn't let them touch until it was time for dessert.

To anyone peeking in, Larinda mused, they might have been one happy little family. She imagined herself with her own little family someday, the one her parents so fervently wished she'd get started on, the one the hurricane had made seem so important now. Putting a face other than Cash's on her imaginary husband, however, didn't work. Only Cash's features would fit.

For the first time in her life, Larinda heard and felt her biological clock tick. There was no mistaking it. At twenty-eight there was no rush to have children, but this logic couldn't quell her longing for a family of her own.

She slid the casserole into the oven. Cash didn't quite fill the bill as a husband, anyway. She could never marry a man who didn't know and love movies, for one thing, and her ideal man was not dark haired but blond.

She had also never imagined herself marrying anyone who'd been married or had a child. It should have been difficult to imagine Cash as her husband—and lover. It wasn't.

She tore lettuce leaves into a salad bowl, and added radishes and cucumber. If they were a family, she and Cash would tuck Dan into bed and then settle down to watch a TV program. Later, she and Cash would go to bed together and . . .

She felt the color rise on her cheeks as she imagined what would happen then. Cash would kiss her as he had last night. He would also kiss her as he hadn't last night, moving down from her mouth to her body. In bed, between the sheets, he would swell and rise to her stroking hands.

"Timberrr," he would whisper much later, in their finest moment together. She shivered.

"Larinda? Knock-knock. Anyone there?" she heard him say from the table.

She jumped. "What? Yes." She didn't dare turn around with her cheeks aglow.

"How much longer before dinner?"

"Not long," she mumbled, tossing cherry tomatos into the salad. "Why don't you two finish up and set the table?"

She had her wandering mind under control by the time she served dinner. The family she'd imagined having was the last thing she wanted right now. She wanted, *needed*, every shred of the security she'd lost. That meant having Outlaw Video.

Or did it mean bringing the Moonglow back to its former glory until she could afford Outlaw Video? Why did that nebulous idea keep tugging at her?

"Before you know it," Cash said across the table, "you'll be headed south and we'll be back to soup and sandwiches here."

"And store cookies," Dan added. "Did Mom ever bake cookies, Dad?"

Cash cleared his throat. "No, she—" he stabbed his fork at a tomato in his salad "—wasn't the type."

As much as he wanted to, he didn't dare cast a glance Larinda's way to check her reaction to Dan's mention of Rita. He didn't like how grateful he felt for the feast Larinda had made of the simple ingredients in his kitchen. He knew he'd be better off to ignore wanting what Rita had never been: a loving woman in his home, warming his heart and his hearth.

But Larinda—cookies and casseroles aside—wasn't that woman. Give Ms. Outlaw Video her way and she'd have him jobless in no time. He'd warmed his heart at the wrong fire once already and gotten burned to a crisp. He wouldn't be fool enough to repeat that mistake.

That didn't mean he'd refuse second helpings of dinner and dessert tonight, though. Rita's way to his heart sure as hell hadn't been through his stomach. She had never roused a tender streak in him, either, as Larinda had last night.

She was desirable, no doubt about that. And judging by the heat of her response last night, she was as sexually frustrated as he was. He knew from life in a rough logging town—and Rita—that sex could be as simple as scratching an itch between two consenting adults.

He was itching to know if Larinda was a redhead all over. Later tonight, he decided, he'd try to find out.

TWO HOURS LATER, Larinda had bowled the lowest score in the entire bowling alley. And Cash had decided not to make any moves on her. That damned indomitable spirit of hers had changed his mind. Even as she'd gamely bowled her last gutter ball, she'd been down but not out.

"Next time," she had assured him, Dan and herself after each miss, "I'll get it right."

She had been generous, too, cheering his and Dan's strikes although they made her performance seem even worse by comparison. More than once Cash had felt like wrapping his arms around her and telling her she didn't have to get anything right for him to admire her grit and tenacity.

"I wasted every cent you spent on my game," she lamented during the drive home.

No comment came from the back seat, for Dan had curled up and fallen asleep there. "Dinner was worth a week of bowling. I haven't eaten well since I left home to get married. Rita, my ex-wife, didn't know a kitchen from a linen closet."

Larinda shrugged. "I'm not all that domestic, either. I know food from working in the deli, that's all. Besides, it was only tuna casserole." She let a moment pass. "When was your divorce?"

"Dan was two when she left. It was a short story. She got pregnant, we got married, everyone said it wouldn't work and they were right." He shrugged. "You ever been married?"

"No." Reluctant to explain the reasons why, she asked, "Why isn't Dan with your ex-wife?"

"She was as unmotherly as she was undomestic. My mother did day care until I came here."

"You lived at home?"

"No. I had my own house. I sold it to my youngest stepbrother before I left."

"You're not in such dire straits as you represented when you refused my offer, then?" Larinda inquired, stiffening.

Behind the wheel, Cash also went rigid. "That depends on how you look at it. Selling out in Oregon gave me bucks enough for a down payment on a house in these parts, but that's all. I won't be able to buy here in Weston unless I can score a steady income after you put me out of business."

"With money in the bank, you're in better shape than *I* am, Cash."

"You have only yourself to support. I have Dan. And now I have only one year on my lease instead of the two I wanted. Furthermore—"

She made a face and cut him short with a wave of her hand. "Don't say I can always live in the trailer and work in Weston until your lease expires. I heard you the first time."

"And ignored me," he added. "Quit making me the villain here. You'll have your insurance money soon enough."

Larinda crossed her arms over her chest. "I wish I hadn't baked those cookies for *your* benefit tonight. For Dan's, yes, but not yours."

Cash retorted, "*I* wish I hadn't eaten them. They're giving me indigestion."

"They were dee-licious," Dan sleepily murmured from the back seat. "The best."

Larinda hunched down in front, abashed that she'd flared up without thinking of Dan back there. A glance at Cash revealed he felt the same way. She stared ahead, her lips pressed tightly together.

It was bad enough that Cash was stubborn. It was worse that he'd been withholding information. She'd trusted that he'd been open and honest about his situation. It was a blow to learn that he'd been neither. It hit her where she was weakest, where her trust in men had already been undermined twice.

Tomorrow couldn't come soon enough as far as she was concerned. The farther she got from Cash Bowman the happier—and safer—she'd be.

Cash drove in silence wondering how he could have let her even *touch* his precious car two days in a row, much less tempt his heart that night in the wind. As for giving her a tumble tonight, no way, babe. He wasn't that hard up. She could clear the hell out tomorrow and take her cookie recipe with her. She couldn't get far enough fast enough for him.

For a fleeting moment, Larinda felt tempted to really fire his rockets by threatening to fix up the Moonglow to show movies. If he dared her to try, it would be a financial risk to back up the threat with action. No, the heat of the moment was no time to test that idea. Not even on Cash.

She had to get away from him and back to Anaheim to consider her options. He could make her so mad she couldn't think. It made her seethe that he hadn't mentioned the asset of his house sale before this. Now, in addition to being infuriating and inflexible, he couldn't be trusted. She had to wonder what else he was keeping to himself.

And she had kissed him last night! At first she'd been vulnerable to the tenderness he'd shown, then too sensually aroused to resist kissing him. She had regretted it ever since. Then again, he'd been open, vulnerable and aroused, too. She had kissed enough men in her life to know.

Indeed, she had loved two of them. Unlike Cash, both had adored movies. Unlike him, both had been blond. She shouldn't have trusted either of them—or Cash.

Cash steered the car into the carport behind his trailer. He cut the engine and glanced into the back seat. "Looks like my star bowler needs a lift into bed. Give me a hand with the door?"

Larinda helped him with the car door, the trailer door and Dan's bedroom door. While Cash got Dan into pajamas and bed, she scoured and rinsed the casserole dish and cookie sheet she'd left to soak in the sink. She was towel-drying the glass dish when Cash came out.

"Dan says good-night," he muttered. "So do I." He stretched out a hand for the towel and dish. "I'll do that."

She relinquished both to him. "Good night. For the last time, I might add."

The dish slipped from his fingers and broke in half at her feet. He swore at the same instant she did. She bent at the same time he did to pick up the pieces.

As she rose with half of the dish in her hand, she remembered the champagne Cash had dropped the first morning in her trailer. He'd looked so rugged and rakish. So . . . romantic.

Standing up with his half, Cash remembered how Larinda had charged at him, brandishing her boot, in her trailer. She'd looked so surprised and sleep softened. So . . . sexy.

"Don't look at me like that," she murmured.

"Don't look at *me* like that," he returned.

"I'm not."

"Neither am I."

Her fingers tightened on the broken dish. "Where shall I put this?"

"After you slice me to bits with it?" His lips twisted. "I can see how much you'd like to."

"Where do you want it, Cash? It's your kitchen."

"Only for a year. Where do I contact you during that time if I have to? Anaheim?"

"Where else? I can see you're not dying for me to continue living next door."

"No one's stopping you, Red."

"If you call me 'Red' one more time, Cash, I *will* slice you to ribbons with this. Where should I put this?"

"In the sink." He turned to slide the piece of dish into it.

She did the same, saying, "I won't be over for breakfast in the morning."

"Since I have to open the market, how do you plan to go pick up your van?"

"If Walt can drop me at the garage on his way home, I'll leave from there."

"It's right on his way." Cash suddenly felt empty at the thought of her leaving. With her staying next door and sharing meals at his table, he'd felt less . . . less lonely, damn it. "So," he said, as if he didn't care, "this is our last round in the ring together."

"This is it." She suddenly felt hollow at the idea of not seeing Cash until the lease expired. A year. Who would soothe her fears when a storm struck? "You've been—" she softened her tone for the final thanks she owed him "—very helpful."

"I've had my moments," he agreed more mildly than before. "If not for Dan, I might have entertained your offer. Who knows?"

"You could still entertain it, Cash," she said, hope springing up. "I haven't withdrawn the offer."

He shook his head. "I admire your spirit and persistence, though. I really do." He watched the sudden light in her face die, saw the faintest glisten of tears in her brown eyes. "Hey," he said softly, "don't."

"I won't. Tears have never gotten me anything I wanted." She lifted her chin. "I won't give in to them now."

"Maybe not, but you'll be leaving mad."

"Could *you* go with a smile if you'd come here with high hopes and seen them die?"

"You could give it a try." *Smile*, he felt like saying. *Just once more before you go.* He couldn't say that. But there was nothing to prevent him from reaching out and twining a lock of her tempting hair around his finger. "You could try remembering the good parts."

"Don't, Cash," she said.

He heard a quaver in her voice. "Why? Because you'd rather go away mad? Or because you're afraid of a goodbye kiss?"

"Because I'd like to leave without . . . last night happening again."

"It was strong stuff, Red." He lifted his finger to tilt her chin up higher. "Too strong to keep it from happening again, if you ask me."

She licked her lips. A last kiss with a double edge—an edge of anger and an edge of tenderness—would be a fitting finale to the tug-of-war they'd waged with each other. From the very first she had experienced a clash of emotions where he was concerned. Yet she wanted to feel his lips on hers one last time.

"Cash, there's no point."

"No point in what? In kissing goodbye and leaving it at that?"

"Exactly. We're business associates. A handshake would be more fitting, wouldn't it?"

"After last night?" He shook his head. "I don't think so. Neither do you, by the way you're looking at me."

Larinda couldn't deny it. Not when he cupped her chin in his palm or when he sank his lips upon hers. Certainly not when lightning struck and she curled her arms tight around his neck and he wound his around her middle.

Cash drove his hands into the vivid excess of her hair where it cascaded down her back. Though he couldn't have said at that instant what he truly wanted with her, he did know what he didn't want: a one-night stand.

Maybe he wanted to mean something positive to her instead of something negative? She had rattled his emotional defenses during her short stay. He felt more than just physical attraction for her.

He'd known passion with Rita but never a sudden, bottomless need for connection. At this moment, nothing would feel more right than the union of their two bodies. Although his swelling sex told him he needed sexual contact, the swell of need in his heart made all the difference.

Larinda shifted her body, yearning to press more intimately against Cash. How seductive his tongue was, mating with hers in slow, sleek strokes. Yet there was something tender and wistful in his deepening kiss. He'd begun to care, she realized. He was communicating it and his silent message made all the difference. It made what was happening more than physical.

Oh, more of this and she'd lose control. He was a man; he'd take whatever she gave. And he was losing no time now. He was gliding his lips from her mouth to her throat as he murmured incoherent words against her skin.

She felt him lift her and settle her bottom on the kitchen counter. The heels of her boots brushed against the cupboard doors below it. Then the hem of her denim skirt slid up as he spread her knees and made space for his hips between her thighs.

"Yes," he whispered against the neckline of her cotton pullover. His hands left her bared knees and rose to her breasts. He pulled back a little, looked straight into her eyes. "I wanted you the minute you walked into my office. I wanted to tangle my hands in your hair and have you right there on my desk."

"Cash—"

"If that shocks you, Red, it should. It shocked *me*." He closed his eyes and circled his thumbs over the peaked tips of her breasts. "The other night when I covered you up with my sleeping bag...all I could think about was getting under it with you. Like this." He slid his hands beneath her cotton pullover.

Larinda gasped. "This can't go where it's leading. It—"

"It can go wherever we want." He unhooked her bra and cradled the smooth weight of her breasts in his palms. "We're both willing."

"We shouldn't be. Oh, Cash," she moaned as his fingertips whispered over her bare skin.

He moaned, too, feeling her nipples swell and rise at his touch. He circled his thumbs again and again over her nipples and outlined her parted lips with his tongue.

Larinda, had never experienced such an intense, immediate response to any man in her life. It hurt to want Cash so much. She felt a sweet ache where he kissed, where he caressed, where his straining zipper rubbed between her spread thighs. She inched forward on the counter and moved with the friction.

Her response made Cash crazy—and reckless. He pushed her skirt up to her waist, drew her sweater and bra up and off. He gathered her hair forward to frame her pale breasts with its waves and tendrils.

"A forest fire in the night," he murmured, running his fingers down the length of her hair. Bending his head, he kissed the berried crest of each breast.

Larinda arched back, uttering a small cry as Cash took her nipples into his mouth. Twining her legs around his hips, she dropped her head back and rested it against the upper cupboard. Here was what she had fantasized from the moment she'd first seen him. His hands in her hair, his mouth against her skin, his body hard and urgent against hers. Countless times she had indulged in the fantasy.

She had never imagined them in a kitchen, though. That happened in movies—like *Bull Durham*—more than in real life. Yet this was no movie. It was reality, happening so fierce and fast that there was no chance to think of slowing down.

She wasn't thinking now in any coherent way. Minutes ago she had been furious with this man. Now she felt only a fury of need to hold him closer, closer. Now she felt only...oh, the strong suction of his mouth, the sensuous descent of his hand to the place that throbbed between her thighs. His fingers moved there, inched under the inner leg of her panties.

"Dad? Are you still up?"

Cash's mouth and hands froze the same instant Larinda went still. He drew back from her breast and cleared his throat. Dan's bedroom door, thank goodness, was closed.

"Yeah." Cash swallowed. "Still up. Uh...bad dream wake you up, Dan?"

"Nope. A good one."

"You need a drink of water or, uh, something?"

"Nope. 'Night, Dad."

"'Night," Cash called back. Then he buried his face between Larinda's breasts and blew out a long, ragged sigh. "First time I've ever forgotten about Dan. Jeez, he could've wandered out and . . ." He withdrew his hand from where it still touched her intimately.

Larinda thawed out of her sudden freeze. Her ankles unlocked behind Cash. Her knees fell away from him. Her arms loosened their possessive embrace of his torso.

"I forgot, too," she whispered. "Hand me my sweater."

Cash pulled back, still holding her around the waist. His gaze roved over her face, her breasts, her bare thighs and booted calves. "Shame on us."

"Yes. My sweater, Cash."

He didn't move. Only his hungry eyes moved, as they roamed over her exposed body.

"Cash..."

Grimacing, he slowly bent and retrieved her sweater and bra from the floor. "Guess it's the end of the line for us," he said. He looked rueful as she hooked the front catch of her bra.

"The end," she confirmed, pulling her knit top down over her head. "Just like in the movies."

Not quite the end, though. They remained as they'd been, Larinda seated on the counter, Cash secure in the valley of her thighs. He couldn't resist pressing the hardest part of himself against her one last time. Rotating his hips, he made his need for her explicit.

"What have we been so spitting mad at each other about since you came to Weston?" he muttered.

Larinda had to search her memory for a moment. "The lease," she murmured back. "You won't sell out so that I can sell out. I refuse to give you two years on your lease. Remember?"

"I forgot my own son, remember?"

Other things too important to forget for long were filtering back into her brain, as well. Things she had lost her grip on in his arms. She had flung reason aside and let her responses to Cash take over. For long, hot, heady minutes she had forgotten she couldn't trust Cash. She'd also forgotten what she really wanted and who was preventing her from having it.

There was so much she should have kept in mind, so much she had let slip. Cash was the barrier to what she valued above all: financial security, independence, the ability to work for herself. He hadn't been aboveboard about his tidy sum in the bank. Most disturbing, she had let herself forget that Cash was still as keen as ever to have two years instead of one on his lease.

And here she was, pelvis to pelvis with him, as if none of it mattered. Being so intimate, so open, could start him thinking she had a weakness for him and that she might weaken in other ways. She didn't want him thinking that.

"Cash, stop. Let me stand."

"Larinda, I—"

"Back off. Please."

He backed away, trailing her hair between his fingers. The sudden, closed look on her face made him clam up, too. He was abruptly aware that he shouldn't have shown such weakness. It could put in question the strength of his mental resolve.

A woman could use a man's sexual weaknesses to manipulate him, he reminded himself. He didn't want Larinda thinking the heat of a moment might change his mind about anything they'd discussed.

Larinda clamped her knees together and slid off the counter. She expected her legs to support her, yet they buckled.

Cash caught her up by the shoulders. "See you next year," he whispered.

"On the dot," she assured. Pulling out of his arms, she stepped around him toward the door.

Cash kept his back to her. After he heard the door slam shut behind her, he looked down at his strained zipper. Good thing Larinda would be leaving tomorrow.

6

LARINDA HAD NO TROUBLE waking early the next
morning, for she had slept fitfully. At first light, she
dressed, shouldered her canvas tote and left her trailer
to track down Walt Whitman for the ride she needed.
She found him watching the sun rise over the high,
sagging fence that enclosed the Moonglow.

"Cash told me you need a lift to get your van," he
said. "I'm available."

"He's already up and working?"

Walt shook his head. "Up, maybe, but not at work
yet. I ran into him last night. Actually, it was around
two this morning. He was out polishing that jewel of a
car Chester left him. Said sleep wasn't his best friend."

That explained why an outdoor light had gone on
last night in Cash's backyard, Larinda thought. She had
stared at the lit square of her bedroom window for quite
some time. She hadn't gotten out of bed to peek at him,
though. If she'd seen that his frustration equaled hers,
she might have gone out to finish with him what they'd
started.

"You want to speak to him before we're on our way?"

"No." Larinda followed Walt to his car.

"Too bad about this old place," he said again as he
drove through the gate. "Cash says you won't be fixing
it up for movies. He's happy about that, of course. He'd
have to work mighty hard if you did."

"It's an intriguing idea nevertheless," she allowed.

He nodded. "You considering it at all?"

"Not seriously, Walt."

Down the road from the Moonglow they passed a hayfield where several workers were erecting the framework for a big billboard. Walt slowed the car. "There's a sign of the times for you," he commented. "A big land developer just bought this parcel of land to build houses. A lot of Westonians want to buy—including Cash."

Larinda frowned. "I asked Cash once about development in this area and he shrugged it off. This land has been bought up?"

"Some of it. Cleve Davis, the developer, has the town council close to sold on the zoning he needs to get the bulldozers going out here."

"The council must be totally sold if he's putting up a sign," Larinda said.

Walt shrugged. "You know these developer types. They'll put the cart before the horse if they think they can get away with it."

"Walt, this means I could sell the Moonglow for land value without much effort, doesn't it?"

"None at all," Walt affirmed. "If farmers don't want to sell—and there're some real diehards out here—then what land Davis *can* get his hands on is worth a pretty penny to him."

Larinda craned around for a last look before Walt sped up again. "That means I could sell right now, for a handsome profit, if only Cash would . . ." She trailed off, her expression grim from more than lack of sleep. Cash had kept a lot to himself the day she'd quizzed him about Davis Development. He couldn't be trusted any farther than a bat could see.

"Cash told me about the lease and your offer," Walt volunteered. "Chester would probably have taken it, but not Cash. He saw too much go down the tubes in the timber industry up north to be looking out for anyone but himself and Daniel."

"Well, *I* saw enough go down the tubes with the hurricane to be looking out for anyone but me, Walt."

He gave her a sympathetic smile. "I hear you. What do you plan to do until you can sell?"

"I don't know." She drummed her fingers on the armrest. "The only true roof I have over my head, if I want it, is the trailer back at the Moonglow. I wonder if it could be moved elsewhere?"

"You'd have to pay rent space elsewhere," Walt observed. "Why pay when it's free on your property?"

"Cash and I haven't found much we can agree about in the past few days. I doubt we'd be good neighbors for the next year."

"Little Dan could use a neighbor like you," Walt said with an eloquent glance her way. "Cash keeps as close an eye as he can on him, of course, but he's stretched thin as a single parent. He's trying to accomplish too much in too short a time now that the lease is expiring sooner than he'd expected."

"Walt, I'd give him more time on his lease if I could. I can't. He must have told you I had to borrow to have the van repaired."

"He did tell me you aren't sitting pretty. Yep." Walt winked and grinned. "*I* told him you were the prettiest woman Weston had ever seen. Except for my wife, Fran, that is."

Hearing that name, Larinda recalled her first few moments at the Moonglow. "Francine Marie wouldn't be her name, would it?"

"Sure would." He winked again. "When I told her Cash's new landlady was a redhead, she remembered you asking for Chester."

Larinda sighed, then managed a smile. "My hair does make an impression."

"Made the biggest one on Cash," he said as he turned into the garage parking lot. "If anyone bothered to ask, I'd say he's not overjoyed to see you go."

Larinda gave him a sharp glance.

He acknowledged it with a small smile. "I hear you. Now, where's this van of yours?"

Larinda surveyed the assorted vehicles parked in the lot. "I don't see it."

"Maybe I'd better not leave just yet in case you might be needing a ride back without it."

Larinda gritted her teeth. "I'm sure they're just finishing it up."

That wasn't what Lonnie had to say. He had the phone receiver to his ear when she approached the service desk. He put it down.

"I was just ringing you. Like I told you the other day, the flu bug's hit my boys hard here. Me, too, matter of fact." He ran a hand over his pale face. "I'm running on empty. The van . . ." He spread his hands.

Larinda wanted to rant and rave. She wanted to demand her van *now*, without delay. She wanted to give Lonnie and the flu bug a big, shrill piece of her mind. But how could she chew out a man in his condition? He looked very green around the gills.

She slumped against the service desk. "When do you think she'll be ready, Mr. Lonsdale?"

"Late this afternoon? She's three-quarters fixed."

"Will she be over or under the estimate?" Larinda inquired wearily.

"Right on the nose. To the penny."

"Good." Her father had sent just that much. To the penny. "I'll be here late this afternoon."

He gave her a wan smile. "I hear you inherited the old drive-in," he remarked before she trudged away. "Any chance you'd be fixing it up for movies?"

LARINDA REFLECTED UPON Lonnie's words as Walt dropped her off at the Moonglow gate. Weston certainly had a keen interest in seeing the Moonglow back in the movie business again. She plucked up her courage and headed for the check-in booth to let Cash know he hadn't seen the last of his landlady yet.

"Lonnie must be late with the van," he observed dryly when she got there. "How long?"

"Late afternoon. He promised."

"Want to earn breakfast and lunch?"

"What starving beggar would say no? Doing what?"

"Taking care of Dan. He woke up this morning with the same bug Jeffie caught. Upset stomach. Fever. Mrs. Soames is keeping an eye on him right now. She didn't come here to baby-sit, though." He gestured at the line of vendors. "Just my luck I've got the biggest check-in I've ever had on a weekday."

"I'm all Dan's," she assured him.

"Thanks. I'll start calling baby-sitters as soon as I can." Cash watched her hurry off, then break into a run toward the trailer. For the first time that morning, he breathed easy. He didn't like it that Larinda was the source of his relief, but with Dan sick, he didn't care to speculate about it.

In Cash's trailer, Larinda found Mrs. Soames crocheting a toaster cover at top speed while watching a morning game show on TV.

"Poor sick little tyke," Mrs. Soames said, shaking her head. "He's asleep. Cash didn't look too good himself when he asked me to watch Dan. Worried, you know."

"Of course." Larinda was worried, too. Dan was a special little guy, so easy to love. "I can stay with him until later in the day, Mrs. Soames."

"You'll stay longer than that," Mrs. Soames said, gathering up her yarn and crochet hooks. "And you won't be away from here long after you leave, you know."

Larinda remembered the honey farmer saying Mrs. Soames had second sight. She hoped it wasn't true.

The old woman dashed that hope by adding, "I'm psychic on my mother's side of the family, so I know. Not that I go around telling folks all I see out in the spiritual ozone, mind you. But you look like you could use advance notice."

"Thank you, but I'll be leaving late this afternoon as soon as my van is repaired down at Lonsdale's."

Mrs. Soames smiled in cheery disbelief, her hand on the doorknob. "Leave Danny boy in the care of some stranger he's never met? No, that's not how you operate, Larinda Outlaw. Your van will be ready when Lonnie said it would, but you're going to bide by that motherless boy—and his lonesome dad—longer than you think."

Unwilling to dispute the claim of an elder of the community, Larinda shrugged and gave her a non-committal smile. "We'll see."

Mrs. Soames left, but not without the last word. "Seeing's believing, I always say."

Larinda tiptoed into Dan's room to check on him. His face was flushed as he slept and he was breathing uneasily. Her heart went out to him. He stirred a little as she touched her fingers to his hot, freckled cheek.

"Shh," she whispered. "Sleep, Danny...sleep." It was as easy now as it had been last night for her to care for him as though he were her own child. How could his mother have abandoned him?

As she tiptoed out of the room, she reflected that Mrs. Soames might be right. Leaving Dan sick—and Cash to worry himself sick—wouldn't be easy. But what were baby-sitters for? Cash would find someone willing to care for Dan and she would leave this afternoon as planned.

She made coffee and cold cereal for herself and put canned chicken-noodle soup on to warm should Dan wake up. Settled at the table, she glanced through the local newspaper and ate her breakfast. *The Westonian* was full of Weston news and business advertising. She saw an ad for the flea market. Slick and eye-catching, it proclaimed Cash as owner-manager of the operation.

But she was owner of the property. Property that Cleve Davis would just love to snap up. In the real-estate section she spotted a Davis Development ad. "Top dollar," it read, "for vacant land."

She closed her eyes, gritting her teeth. One bulldozer could make the Moonglow vacant land in no time. Why had Jethro stipulated in the will that she couldn't sell the drive-in or even negotiate a sale until Chester's lease expired? All because Chester had saved Jethro's life a lifetime ago?

She had to concede that it did make sense. Owing Chester so much, Jethro wouldn't have wanted him to be out of a home and a job at his age without adequate notice. Jethro just might have hoped his goddaughter would bring the Moonglow back to its former glory as a drive-in. Hadn't the attorney mentioned Jethro's undying affection for the place? Yes, he had.

Larinda closed the paper. She washed and dried her breakfast dishes and those Cash had left. That done, she tidied up the rest of the trailer, including Cash's bed. She picked up one of his pillows and fluffed it. Unable to resist, she lifted the pillow to her nose and breathed deep. Cash. The scent of his hair and skin was as distinctive as he was. She detected no hint of perfume, no lingering evidence of a female. As the night watchman's wife, Fran had to be right about Cash sleeping alone.

Larinda breathed deeper, savoring his scent. Last night, if Dan hadn't interrupted, she might have shared this pillow with Cash. Would he have taken her to his bed with his son so nearby? Yes, she decided, and she'd have gone with him. She wouldn't have slept here, but she would have been intimate with Cash.

She set the pillow aside and smoothed the rumpled sheets. It was here that she would have opened herself completely to Cash, felt his skin sliding over hers, his mouth kissing everywhere.

With heart beating faster, she drew the blanket up. Was he as exciting a lover as his kisses and caresses last night had promised? Her fingers trembled as she pulled the forest green bedspread over the blanket. Was he everything she had fantasized he would be? She fluffed his other pillow tempted to lift it to her face again. Cash.

"Larinda?" he said in a loud whisper from the doorway.

She whirled around, clutching the pillow to her breast. Cash filled the doorway, made it look far smaller than when she had passed through it. His eyes were a darker gray-blue than she'd ever seen.

"You startled me," she got out.

"I was afraid I'd wake Dan," he murmured. He glanced at the pillow she clutched. "What are you doing?"

"Just—" she dropped the pillow close to where it belonged "—earning breakfast and lunch with housework. The bathroom's next on my list. What are *you* doing?"

"Checking on Dan." *And you.* The thought of Larinda tucking his bedsheets and plumping his pillows was enough to make him want to shut his bedroom door and lock himself in with her. He should have done it last night. He backed away from temptation now.

"I thought it best to let Dan sleep," Larinda said, dusting her hands on her skirt as she came around the bed.

Cash nodded and stepped aside to let her pass. "I agree."

He followed her to the bathroom, where she began straightening the towels he had left bunched over the shower door and towel bar. "You don't have to do my housework, Red," he said from the doorway.

"Yes, I do. I'll go stir-crazy otherwise. And don't— repeat, *do not*—call me 'Red.'" She shook out a bath towel and folded it before draping it neatly where it belonged.

"All I need is for you to be here for Dan."

"I'm here." Larinda continued folding and hanging. "Have you given him anything to bring his temperature to normal?"

"Children's Tylenol. He couldn't keep it down."

"When he wakes, I'll try again." She frowned at the soap-spotted mirror above the washbasin. "What do you do while you shave? The twist, the jerk, and the Watusi?"

"One right after the other," he confirmed with a sarcastic rise of one eyebrow. "Buck naked. You should see me."

"I'll pass." She wiped the driest of the towels over the mirror, trying to erase from her mind the image his comment was conjuring up. It would help if he'd back his broad shoulders and narrow hips out of the doorway and return to tending his market. That way she could stop thinking about how he must look shaving in the nude.

He didn't back out. He stayed there, silently watching her, wishing she hadn't so easily dismissed his offer to see his bare body. A hesitant reply would have confirmed his suspicion that she'd been lifting his pillow to her nose to get a whiff of him. He wished he'd waited to see if she would do it before he'd spoken up.

He knew that when he reclaimed the bed linens in the other trailer, he wouldn't be able to resist the opportunity. He'd fill his lungs with her scent, just as he was filling his eyes with the sight of her right now.

Damn her leave-a-man-crazy hair, her leave-him-wild breasts, her leave-him-hurtin'-for-certain thighs. After weakening to her charms last night, he was desperate to see her out of his sight and his life. But after making phone calls to ten baby-sitters and two child-care agencies in his office, he was equally desperate to see her stay as long as Dan was sick.

"Would you spend another day or two here?" he forced himself to ask.

Larinda kept her eyes on the mirror, knowing what could happen if she stayed. "Why?"

"I can't get a sitter for Dan." He gripped the door frame with his hands and explained about the calls he'd made in vain. "Two weren't booked, but they wouldn't take on a kid with the flu."

"There must be someone," Larinda said, shaking her head against the plea she heard in his voice. Hearing it was bad enough. If she looked at him, she might give in to the plea she'd surely see in his eyes. Damn his eyes. He had only to look at her for some essential part of her brain to go goofy. She scrubbed with great zeal at a speck on the mirror.

"I'll pay the going rate for day care if you'll stay," he prompted. "I'll also keep calling sitters, but if no one can come . . . you're all I've got until closing time."

That would be later than late afternoon, Larinda knew. Too late for her to leave for Anaheim? No. She could drive all the way in the dark. What would Cash do beyond tonight if she left? He had an exam at school tomorrow, if she remembered correctly.

"You do need what I'd pay you to stay, Larinda."

The husky catch she heard in his voice made her look at him. That look was her downfall. "Pay me whatever's fair, then," she relented.

"You'll stay?"

She nodded. "Call the garage and tell Lonnie not to rush, would you? He's got the flu, too, poor guy. I'll call my parents."

"Great." It was all Cash could do not to hug and kiss her and say he'd pay double the going rate for her time. He took one step forward, then two back. He'd better get lost before she changed her mind. "I'll phone Lonnie, and . . . thanks, Larinda. A bunch."

After Cash hustled out, Larinda had to stare herself down in the mirror until the goofy expression wiped itself off her face.

"None of this is because Mrs. Soames knows something you don't," she lectured at her reflection. "You're staying because Dan needs you, and you need every cent Cash will pay. There is no such thing as the 'spiritual ozone.'"

There was, however, the need to wash the clothes she wore if she'd be staying. They were long past fresh. It was a good thing Cash had a washer and dryer. Maybe she'd throw the bathroom towels in to make a full load.

A tug on her wrist cut her thoughts short. Dan stood there, his feverish little face looking up at her. "I'm gonna urp again," he said. And he did.

IT WAS MIDAFTERNOON before Cash checked on Dan again. He stepped quietly into Dan's bedroom and found Larinda propped up against the headboard of his son's bed, asleep. Dan, also asleep, was cradled in her arms.

Looking at them, Cash got a lump the size of a clenched fist in his throat. In that moment, he saw how much Dan needed a mother as well as a father. Shaken, Cash backed away to the kitchen.

In the sink he saw two soup bowls with evidence of chicken-noodle soup and crackers in them. It heartened him to hope that Dan was holding some nourishment down as he slept. It made him feel even better to know his son was being given the tender, loving care he deserved.

It hurt, though, that he couldn't close the market and tend to Dan himself. He vowed that tomorrow he'd skip his classes after his exam first thing in the morning. For that stretch of time, Larinda would be an enormous help. If Dan was still sick the day after tomorrow, she would be an even bigger help. And if she made dinner tonight . . .

Cash pulled out a chair and sat down at the table. If she made dinner tonight he'd get down on his knees and thank her. Until she arrived, he hadn't been aware of needing help so much.

Last night he'd wanted Larinda's help less than he'd wanted her body. It wasn't hard for him to admit that he'd been lonely for sex for a long time. It was harder to accept that Larinda seemed to be the only woman he wanted.

He looked up as Larinda walked in, rubbing the sleep from her eyes.

"Oh." She faltered. "When did you get here?"

Cash stood. "I was just leaving. How's Dan?"

"Better." Larinda slid into a chair across the table. "He's weak, but he's keeping a cracker and a small bowl of soup down."

Cash held still for a moment, focusing his eyes on the soft curve of her lips.

"His fever has broken," she added.

Cash struggled against the urge to say *Mine hasn't.* It took him a second to win out over it. "That's good."

"What would you like for dinner after you close the market tonight?"

"You don't have to cook—"

She held up a hand. "Macaroni and cheese? Fruit salad on the side?"

He shrugged, careful not to look as if his mouth was already watering. "Whatever you feel like dishing up. I'll be here." Turning, he left.

"I'll be here, too," Larinda sighed after the door shut. "Longer than I think, if the 'spiritual ozone' has any substance to it."

7

CONTRARY TO his earlier impulse, Cash didn't get down on his knees and thank Larinda for the delicious meal she made that night. He restrained the urge and ate his fill. After dinner he settled in his easy chair with Dan on his lap and read to him.

Curled up on the couch, Larinda leafed through a news magazine, listening to Cash read from *The Golden Treasury of Natural History* about animals and insects and plants. These, she had already learned, were Dan's favorite things. A budding naturalist, he had nature posters tacked all over his bedroom walls.

After waking late that afternoon, he had shown her the bugs and butterflies he'd collected in the surrounding hayfields. "When I get well," he had promised, "I'll show you where I saw a trap-door spider once." His flu-flushed cheeks had burned brighter with enthusiasm. "And wait till you see the two foxes who live out there. Holy moley, are they neat."

Now Larinda glanced up from her magazine and saw that Dan was heavy eyed and almost asleep. Cash rubbed his cheek against his son's blond curls.

She knew how sweet that affectionate gesture could feel, for she had repeated it many times to comfort Dan that day.

Cash looked up and caught her soft gaze. His voice trailed off. He rested his chin on Dan's curls and smiled.

Larinda blushed. She looked back down at her magazine, turned a page and feigned interest in an advertisement.

Cash closed the book, set it aside and rose from the chair with Dan asleep in his arms. When he came back from Dan's bedroom, he found Larinda at the front door with the magazine in one hand and the other hand on the doorknob.

"Leaving?" he said. *So soon?*

She nodded. "You must have studying to do for tomorrow's exam." Opening the door, she stepped out. "See you in the morning," she added, and she was gone.

Cash slumped into his chair. Scowling, he reached for his textbook. Yes, he did have studying to do. No, he didn't want to do it. He wanted to take Larinda to the bed she had made for him and show her how grateful he felt for every thoughtful thing she'd done today, from feeding Dan soup to doing two loads of laundry. He wanted to make love to her. Tonight.

In her trailer, Larinda stripped and took a cool shower, hoping it would take her mind off Cash. But she stepped out still suffused with emotion and desire, still wanting to be with Cash. In his arms. In his bed. Tonight.

Wrapped in a towel, she dropped down on her bed with a magazine. Flipping page after page, she tried and failed—to concentrate. Finally she tossed it aside and lay back against the pillows. She closed her eyes and visualized Cash, at his kitchen table.

In her mind, he rose from the table . . . left his trailer . . . opened her door . . . walked in to where she lay on the bed . . .

Larinda turned her cheek into the pillow, wishing it were Cash's broad chest. Although she'd often been embroiled in conflict with him, there had been times that she had enjoyed so much. Joking with him as they'd checked in the vendors together on Sunday morning and bowling with him and his son Monday evening had been pleasurable moments. And she wanted to be with him right now.

Gathering the towel around her, she sat up and swung her legs over the edge of the bed. She would go back and visit with him, she decided on impulse. Yes, she'd get back into her skirt, boots and sweater and go over and invite herself in. She'd do what she'd never done before: throw herself at a man. After last night she felt confident that Cash wouldn't throw her out.

Hastily, before she could stem the whim, she dressed, brushed her teeth and hair and left her trailer. The light in Cash's backyard was burning bright.

She ventured around for a look. There he was, passing a chamois polishing cloth over the Chevy's classic rear fender. The convertible top was down, giving the car a sleek, racy look. Cash hadn't spent long studying for his exam, she thought, as she noted the play of his back muscles under his plaid shirt. Maybe he knew the subject well enough that he didn't need to study. Then again, maybe he hadn't studied long for the same reason she hadn't read her magazine.

Hands in her skirt pockets to appear as casual as possible, she approached behind him and inquired, "All done studying?"

He whipped around off balance, with a look of surprise on his face. "Yeah," he replied, regaining his footing. "What brings you out?"

"Just the need for a little fresh air," she lied. It *was* a fine night to be out, after all, not a bit chilly. "And you?"

"The same." He bent to continue wiping the cloth, slower now, over the fender.

Focused on the motion of the chamois instead of on Cash, she sauntered closer. "How's Dan?"

"Deep in dreamland."

"Aren't you worried about him alone inside?"

"Not very. We have a system." He glanced over at Dan's bedroom window. "If I'm out here at night and he needs me, he turns on his lamp. I see his window light up and go inside. It's as safe and easy as being in the next room."

"Bright idea," Larinda agreed. She strolled around the car as if it, and not Cash, was what she'd come to see. "Is this the original upholstery on the seats?"

"My father claimed it is. I'm not up enough on classics to know for sure, but it's definitely in good condition."

She nodded. Her earlier opinion that he was good company was beginning to diminish. He was showing greater interest in his shiny red Chevy than in her.

She felt silly for having ventured out in search of companionship. And even sillier for not knowing what to do now but stand there wondering how to get away gracefully. She took a step toward her trailer.

Cash stopped her by saying from the rear of the car, "That was an ace dinner you cooked tonight. I'll get groceries tomorrow after my exam to replenish supplies. I've decided to skip my other classes to be with Dan."

She postponed her departure. "You'll hardly need a sitter, then."

"I'll need one while I'm gone...if you still don't mind sticking around."

"Without the van I won't be going anywhere," she reasoned aloud with a shrug. Continuing her stroll around the car, she came to the passenger door he'd left open.

"Have a seat," he offered. "Keep me company till I'm through."

She took him up on that offer, settling into the back seat, where she could talk to him more easily. "It's not necessary for you to skip classes tomorrow, you know," she told him. "I *will* be here."

"I don't doubt it."

"Why skip class, then, if you don't have to?"

He stopped the steady swirl of the chamois on the trunk and looked at her. "It did me some good and some bad to see Dan asleep in your arms today. The good was knowing he had the care he should have. The bad was that it should have been *me* holding my sick boy." He resumed his task. "You don't know how a single, working parent misses moments like that."

"No," Larinda murmured, tracing a finger over a seam in the seat upholstery. "I guess I don't. But I can understand how you feel."

"Until you have a child of your own, you can only partly understand."

"Partly, then," she amended. "I hope any child I have is as good and sweet as Dan."

"You don't think he takes after me?" Cash arched an eyebrow her way.

Larinda caught a bantering note in his tone. She matched it. "Not in the least. Not only is his temperament the opposite of yours, so is his hair color."

With a flash of a teasing grin, he accused, "I suppose *you'll* spawn pure redheads, full of spit and fire just like you."

"I am not a salmon," she mocked in a haughty tone. "I will not spawn but give birth to my baby spitfires."

"How many do you plan to have?"

"Plan? I'm not even married."

"How have you managed that?"

"Getting involved with the wrong men is an enormous help. You can't imagine."

"After marrying the wrong woman, I think I can. Do you like being single?"

"Do *you* like it?"

"I asked first."

She considered the question for a second. "I like being my own boss," she decided. "Your turn."

"I'd rather be single than married to Rita."

"There's nothing you miss about it?"

"Nothing but—" he looked up at her "—the physical side of it. Solitude can be a strain."

Larinda saw color graze his cheekbones. She blushed slightly herself and looked away.

"It can be a strain in that sense for anyone," she granted, nervously combing the fingers of one hand through her hair. The conversation had take a sudden, intimate turn.

Cash straightened slowly. He wanted to touch her hair as she was now. He wanted to see it frame her bare breasts again. He wanted to feel it spill over his skin. Oh, the things he wanted to do. More than he'd done last night. What would she say if he turned the light out and got into the back seat with her? What would she do? Bolt out of the car? Or stay?

There was only one way to find out. He pitched the chamois aside and flipped off the light switch on the carport post.

Stunned, Larinda blinked in the darkness. "What—?"

"I'm finished with the car," he said at her ear, "but not with last night. Move over. I'm getting in."

She slid sideways. "Cash, what are you—?" She gasped as he dropped into the seat beside her and pulled her into his arms.

"I'm on fire, Red." He tightened his embrace. "You are, too, or you wouldn't be here. It's not fresh air you came out for, is it?"

She tipped her head back and made out the dark shape of his face so close, so close. "No," she admitted in a shaky whisper, "not entirely."

"That makes two of us. Let's finish last night. Now."

"Here?"

"It's private." He drew her hair back and nuzzled her throat. "Dan won't walk in. I'll keep an eye on his window."

"What about Walt?"

"He called in sick. Flu."

"Even so, Cash, we need protection. I don't have—"

"I do." He leaned over the front seat and popped open the glove compartment, producing two foil squares.

"I need you so much it hurts, Red," he breathed against her lips.

Never before had he called her "Red" and made it sound like an endearment. It sounded like one now. Did he mean it that way?

"Oh, Cash." *Red.* For the first time in her life, it was the sweetest word she'd ever heard.

He sealed his name in her mouth with his and drew her against him. Willing and wanting she went, holding him as tightly as he held her, kissing him as deeply as he kissed her.

She had never made love in a car, didn't know the first thing about it. Cash seemed to know, though. She let him lead the way. He pushed the backs of the front seats to a forward slant with his foot, then eased her down to lie under him on the back seat.

"Pretend we're at a drive-in movie," he murmured, filling his hands with her hair. "What do we care what's on the screen?"

She sifted her fingers through his hair in turn, then traced them trembling over his lips. "I was the kind of girl who cared, remember?"

"I wasn't the kind of boy who did." He slid her sweater up and off and took off his shirt. Drawing the fingers of one hand around the perimeter of her bra cups, he said, "I'm still not."

"You're not a boy, either, Cash."

"No more than you're a girl, Red. We're both consenting adults."

"I've never consented in a back seat." She curved her palms over his shoulders where his muscles bunched, over his chest where dark hair grew thick and springy. "I feel like a very bad girl here with you."

"You don't look like one." His thumb slipped under her bra and rotated the rising peak of one breast. "You look too beautiful to be bad." He tugged on the front clasp of her bra. "Last chance to call it off."

She let him undo the clasp, then drew his hand to her bare breast and lifted her mouth to his. She stroked her thumbs down the sides of his throat and felt the hot beat of his pulse. He made a hoarse, gruff sound when she stroked lower around his nipples. His tongue curled around hers in response, pushing the kiss to the limit. He moved his lips down to her breasts.

His mouth was a wonder, she thought. Everything he did with it made her want to experience more. Eager to feel the rigid thrust of his manhood press between her thighs, she moved under him. "Cash, I'm so turned on..."

"Me, too." He pushed her skirt up and worked her panties off. She helped him, then gasped when he cupped his hand to her. Quivering for him to deepen his touch, she opened herself to him.

With the first dip of his fingers, Cash knew she'd be as sweet to taste as she was to touch. Her soft folds enticed him to delve deeper. Gently, he did so, stroking her female flesh until she let out broken, shivery sighs.

He reveled in the way her hair rippled in thick waves over her bare breasts. Never had he held a woman as erotically exciting as she was. With her skirt riding high, her silky thighs spread, her legs laced around his, she was overwhelmingly erotic.

He sipped a gasp from her lips as he slid one exploring finger into her, tender and deep. He let her set the tempo. Slow. Ahh, that pleased him. He would have long, delicious memories to savor in the days that would stretch ahead without her.

Larinda hadn't known her pleasure would be his inspiration. She hadn't expected his soft murmurs in her ear telling her how wet and tight she was and how good it made him feel to make her feel good. It made her want to give him all she could.

But she could only grip his back with her fingers—she was too swept up by the rhythm of his touch. No bed had ever been so perfect to lie in as the Chevy, no lover as ardent and adept as Cash.

"Cash, please," she pleaded. "Not yet. Not before you're in me."

"You want *me* more than . . . ?"

"More than anything."

"I won't last long, Red. Not the first time."

She pressed her flattened palms against the front of his pants. "You won't have to the first time."

Cash knew then that simple physical need didn't explain everything that was happening tonight. It didn't adequately explain the throaty emotion he'd heard in her request. It didn't account for why he wanted her to know more pleasure with him than she had ever known. Or why he wanted to be the only man in the world to satisfy her every need.

She felt for the button of his fly, freed it and tugged his zipper down. For an instant, she was shocked. No briefs! Fully erect, he surged into her seeking hands. "Oh! My!"

"Easy, Red."

He led her caressing hands to his hips and helped her peel his pants down as far as his knees. Then she helped him roll on a condom. Kneeling above her, he was the most arousingly masculine sight Larinda had ever seen.

He looked down at her waiting for him and touched her again where she was melting and ready. Then he lowered himself to her.

One smooth thrust embedded him deeply. He heard the sound of surrender Larinda made, felt her hands streak down his back to his bare hips and press on them.

"Yes!" She locked her legs around him. "Don't hold back."

He couldn't. She was a hot, pulsing sheath around him, ready to peak, her movements urging him to drive as hard and fast as he wished. He buried his face in her hair, flattened her breasts with the weight of his chest and set the Chevy rocking as passion set the pace.

Breathless and unbridled, Larinda climaxed at the same moment as Cash. As one they let go to each other. As one they shuddered into mindless, mutual release.

Sanity eventually returned, but Larinda couldn't wipe the blissful smile off her lips. Long beyond the last aftershock, she was still savoring the weight of Cash's body upon hers and the way his hand possessively cupped one of her breasts.

Easing up on one elbow, Cash gazed down at her. "Is that a satisfied smile, Red?"

"More satisfied than it's ever been," she had to honestly reply. She touched the up-curved corner of his mouth. "What's this?"

"The same. We're strong stuff together."

"Yes. We are."

Once-in-a-lifetime stuff, he thought. Reluctant to think or say more, he levered higher to check out Dan's window. It was dark, yet he knew he couldn't remain joined to Larinda all night. She felt too perfect under him to part with just yet.

He eased back down and touched soft kisses to her throat and shoulders, telling her how beautiful she was. He told her that her breasts were perfect. He kissed them again, sucked them again, made their centers dark and tight.

Then, somehow, he was harder than before, wanting everything all over again. Larinda enthusiastically complied. They were no less abandoned the second time, and no less syncopated in reaching a second zenith together.

Once in a lifetime is one thing, Cash thought after their hearts had calmed once more. *Twice in a night is something else.* He didn't know what to make of it, didn't want to make too much of it. Yet there it was.

"Red?" He lifted his head from the pillow of her breasts.

"Hmm?"

"Have you . . . ever been . . . uh, simultaneous before this?"

Her fingers stopped slowly stroking his hair. "Have you?"

"I asked first."

"No, I've never been. Not before this."

He pillowed his head again. "Neither have I."

Larinda lay silent and still under him, afraid to speak. This night was more unique and special and memorable than she could ever have expected. She hadn't thought that she could be so compatible with Cash or feel so close to him.

Any closer, Cash thought, and he'd be thinking she was the love of his life. Yes, they'd come twice together. But he couldn't forget that he and Larinda were incompatible in other ways.

Sexual compatibility, Larinda thought, didn't negate the conflicts that still stood between them. Simultaneous orgasms happened all the time in movies. It couldn't be that rare if every Hollywood scriptwriter had written it into a love scene at one time or another. Just because it was rare for herself and Cash, it didn't mean that they had anything special.

Cash disengaged himself with a low groan and sat up. After disposing of the condom, he turned back to stroke Larinda's cheek. "There's probably no hope for finding our missing clothes," he added, tracing the line of her jaw with one finger and trailing it down to the peak of her left breast. To lighten the mood, he teased, "Why does a woman with perfect breasts wear a bra?"

"Why don't *you* wear briefs?"

"Sawdust." He chuckled. "It made me itch worse if I wore them when I logged, so I stopped wearing them except to sleep in. I never got back in the habit."

"Help me find my bra, Cash."

"Why?"

She held his hand still on her. "If you keep touching me there I won't want to put it on and go in. I should go in, you know. You should, too—if only to look in on Dan."

"I know." He felt under himself for her bra and produced it." Here's your sweater, too. Forget my shirt. I'll find it in the morning." Grinning, he dangled a third item of feminine apparel from one finger, just out of Larinda's reach.

"Stop being a tease," she reproved, reaching for her panties. "Give them to me."

"Not yet." He held them away. "I like thinking about you without them."

She pulled her sweater over her head. "Awful man. Hand them over."

"What will you bid? Make me an offer."

"Pancakes for breakfast."

"Not enough. After all, these are silk and lace and French cut. Worth a lot more than pancakes."

"They are not. They're plain, cotton, disaster-relief underwear." She reached again in vain.

"Make me another offer. Something worthwhile." He paused to think, then playfully tossed out, "Like another year on my lease."

Another year on his lease? She knew he was teasing, that he wasn't serious, but it reminded her of one good reason she shouldn't have made love with him. It wasn't the only reason, either. Love required trust, and she couldn't begin to say she trusted him. She couldn't be sure he wouldn't hurt her as she'd been hurt before. Backing away into her corner of the seat, she went still.

Cash saw Larinda looking at him as if he were slowly sprouting horns. He knew that he'd said the wrong thing, but couldn't understand why she was cooling off over a teasing remark. Or maybe he could. Her reaction was an instant reminder to him that they might have bridged one gap tonight, but several more still stretched between them. One big one was that they didn't want the same things in life.

"I hope the lease had nothing to do with this," she said.

He shook his head. "Not for me. What about you, Red?"

Noting the subtle shift away from endearment in that "Red," she coolly replied, "Perhaps we shouldn't have lost our heads out here."

"Maybe not," he agreed. "Before you know it, we'll be suspecting each other of ulterior motives. We'll be accusing each other of adding sex to the bargain."

"We'd both have reason enough if we did, Cash."

"We had reason enough otherwise for what just happened," he contended, adding, "a physical reason, if nothing else."

Larinda felt stung by his curt assessment. "Yes. It was wise to keep emotion out of what just happened, wasn't it?"

"I didn't mean—"

"Putting emotion into it would undoubtedly have ended it in an argument." She heard her tone become brittle. "We have enough to argue about without that, don't we?"

"Red—"

Teeth clenched, she cut in, "I despise that nickname, Cash, and you know it. Give me my underwear. I'm going in."

Scowling, he pitched her panties into her outstretched hand as if they were radioactive. "After you."

He sat there, furious. *Good thing you stuck your foot in your mouth, Bowman*, he congratulated himself. *If you hadn't, think of where you'd be right now. Practically in love. With the wrong woman. You wouldn't want to make the same mistake twice.*

8

LARINDA WOKE UP in a foul mood the next morning. Seeing that the sun had risen bright and shining, she stuck her tongue out at it.

She showered and dressed, waiting until the very last minute before Cash had to leave before showing up at his door.

"Dan's asleep and doing better. Fever's gone," was all Cash said when she reported for duty.

"Good," she replied.

He left without another word and she went directly to the phone. She dialed Lonnie and learned that the van would be ready by noon.

"Can one of your mechanics come out and drive me over to get it?" she asked. "Cash won't be able to when he gets back. His boy is sick."

"I'll come myself," Lonnie said. "Least I can do after the time we've cost you. I'll be there. Noon."

She hung up. Cash would just have to find a baby-sitter if Dan was still feeling too sick for school tomorrow.

She tried not to remember how thrilling Cash's kisses had been the night before. Before everything had gone sour. Before she had realized she'd been had.

She closed her eyes, weakened by memories she couldn't hold at bay. It had been nothing like anything she'd known before. Heaven, to be honest. Ecstasy. She had felt so close to loving him in those precious moments.

And this, she promised herself, was the last time she would remember those moments with Cash.

CASH DROVE from school to the grocery store, then headed home. He knew he'd barely passed his exam. After last night, his concentration was shot. Ten minutes after leaving the Save 'n' Save, he couldn't recall if he'd bought anything or everything he needed. All he could think of was Larinda and what had happened last night to his love life.

Sex life, he amended. However close to love it had seemed to be during certain ecstatic moments, their back-seat tryst had nothing to do with love. But it *had* been better than any sex he'd ever experienced.

He hated wondering what her reaction had been when she'd first looked in her mirror this morning, yet he'd wondered ever since he'd looked into his. Had she done what he'd done? Had she stared at herself, helpless not to relive each kiss and caress, each shudder and sigh? Then had she scowled as he had, and escaped into a cold shower to stop remembering?

He hoped so. He also hoped she'd leave today. A year without her would be a blessing. And a curse. His cold-water bill would go sky high.

Near the Moonglow he passed Cleve Davis's billboard. He realized that Larinda had probably seen it yesterday on her way out. Figuring the less she knew the better, he had neglected to mention Cleve's development plans. He hadn't expected the sign to go up this soon. Maybe it hadn't been up yesterday, since she hadn't said anything yet.

He pulled into the carport, resolving to call Lonsdale's from his office and threaten Lonnie with bodily harm if Larinda's van wasn't ready by noon.

The first thing Larinda said when he walked in with the groceries was "Good news. I'm leaving at noon. The van will be ready then. Lonnie's coming to take me to it. The end."

Cash shoved the dairy products he'd bought into the refrigerator, then checked the kitchen clock. "I can hardly wait. One hour to a happy ending for all concerned."

"I'll be only too glad to wait it out in my trailer," she retorted.

"Before you go, how did Dan do while I was gone?"

"He kept breakfast down," Larinda replied from the door. "He's asleep now. Please tell him good-bye for me when he wakes up."

"With pleasure." He pitched her a candy bar from the grocery bag he was emptying. "One for the road, just in case I owe you something for your time today."

She caught it and sent it hurtling back. "You don't owe me. I didn't make your bed or do anything else domestic today. I just watched cartoons with Dan—" her eyes narrowed "—and wondered why you shrugged off Davis Development the day I asked about it."

He drew apples and iceberg lettuce out of the bag. "What Davis does is his business, not mine."

"Walt tells me you plan to buy one of Davis's houses when they go in down the road."

"What I plan is my business, not Walt's," Cash replied.

Larinda gritted her teeth. "I could sell this land in no time to Davis."

"Not for a year."

"You didn't want me to know a developer was buying land in this area," she accused. "You didn't want me to stay on here and harangue you all year to sell out."

"I did nothing to prevent you from finding out anything you wanted to know."

"You did nothing to share what you knew. You kept it to yourself so I'd go back home and stop bothering you."

"A bother-free year will be a plus after this."

"You simply can't be trusted can you, Cash?"

"Nope. I learned from Rita to play my cards close. Weren't you leaving?"

"I don't have to leave quietly."

"For a sleeping kid's benefit, why don't you try?"

"Only for him would I make the effort. I'll see you in one year—to the day."

"I'll hold you to every minute and second as specified in the lease, Red."

For Dan's sake, Larinda didn't slam the door as she stormed out.

For the same reason, Cash didn't hurl the head of lettuce at the door.

LARINDA FOUND that life in Anaheim hadn't changed in her absence. Disneyland, its world-famous attraction, enchanted young and old alike as it had before her trip to Weston. As it always had been, her parents' deli was too distant from Disneyland to profit from the crowds. A neighborhood crowd was what kept Larry and Linda doing a budget business in submarine sandwiches and oatmeal chewies at Outlaw Deli.

She returned to sleeping on the couch and waitressing in the deli. An extra hand made a big difference, since Larry and Linda ran the place on a shoestring with her brother, Larson, as their only help. It made her nervous how they could happily live month to month with no savings stashed away for a rainy day.

But that was show biz, as far as they were concerned. They'd always lived for the moment, without an eye to the future. Nothing had changed.

On the third day after her return, something changed. Her long-awaited, long-delayed insurance check arrived in the mail. After kissing it a thousand times, she bought a few clothes, a reliable used car and split the cost of the van repair with her father. Banking the rest, she breathed her first sigh of relief since the hurricane.

Returning to the deli from the bank, she sat down in the cramped kitchen for a coffee break with her mother.

"What now?" Linda inquired.

Larinda regarded her plump, blue-eyed mother. "I don't know. Damn that Cash Bowman. If he'd just sell out . . ."

"Since you came back," Linda said, "I get the feeling that more happened between you and Mr. Bowman than a battle over his lease. A battle of the sexes sounds more like it. You haven't been yourself since Weston, Rinda."

"I haven't been myself since Texas, Mom."

Linda shook her head in disagreement. "There's a difference. You wouldn't be in love, would you?"

"In love? With the most stubborn, untrustworthy man I've ever met? I wish I'd inherited the Moonglow free and clear and never met him. The only lovable thing about him is his son, Dan."

"You get soft in the eye whenever you mention either Cash or Dan, Rinda. I see it. Your father and brother see it. It's more serious than you're pretending, isn't it?"

"Not as serious as you and Dad and Larson would like to think."

Larry popped his bald head through the door right then, grinned at his wife and inquired, "Has she confessed, yet?"

"Soon," Linda advised.

Mouth open, Larinda watched his head disappear back out of sight. She looked at her mother. "What is this, a conspiracy?"

"No. We've all simply observed that you've looked homesick since you returned."

Larinda rolled her eyes. "I'm home. How can I be homesick?"

"You look lovesick, as well, Rinda."

"Only because I grew an affection for little Dan while I was there," Larinda said.

"But not for Dan's father?" Linda raised her eyebrows.

"Mom, I know you and Dad would love to see me married and nine months pregnant, but that's not at all practical under the circumstances. I have to get back on my feet again and earn a good living. I want to make up for what I lost."

"A successful business and money in the bank isn't everything, Rinda. It doesn't make up for losing love. Your father and I regret the lean times our family had and that they made you think you need so much now. But you were always loved."

Larinda reached forward and squeezed her mother's hand. "I appreciate that. Always have. I don't know what I'd have done without a family to come home to."

"Remember it when you think about Cash and Dan," her mother said with a wise nod. "Love will hold a couple—and a whole family—together when nothing else can. Love, not money, is the tie that binds."

"I'll remember that when I fall in love, Mom."

"I don't believe for a minute that you aren't in love right now," said Linda. "What are you going to do about it?"

Larinda took what she hoped was a nonchalant sip of coffee. "Even if you're right, I'd do nothing, except *maybe* fix up the Moonglow and show movies for a year until Cash's lease expires."

"Maybe?" Linda's face lit with interest and enthusiasm. "That's a wonderful idea."

Larinda agreed, "Wonderful, but probably not at all feasible."

"Find out, Rinda. Take a few days off and investigate the drive-ins down here in this area."

"Maybe I will, Mom."

"Larry! Larson!" Linda called through the kitchen door. "Come here for a second."

Larry came in, wiping his hands on his apron. Larson, tall, dark haired, blue eyed, followed with a sandwich knife in his hand. "What?" they asked in unison.

"Rinda's going to fix up the Moonglow and show movies, that's what!"

"Wow," said Larry. "Great idea."

"Cool," Larson added.

"I said *maybe*," Larinda protested.

Larson grinned. "Are you only *maybe* in love, too? With Cash Bowman?"

"Not in the least!"

Her mother rose from her seat at the kitchen worktable. "I'll work your deli shift from now on. You get busy calling those drive-ins and talking to the owners. Isn't this exciting? Just like a movie."

LARINDA HELD OUT for two days against calling those drive-ins and talking to the owners. Cash dominated her thoughts in that time. She tried to explain to herself why she'd made love with him, why he'd made love with her. Sexual attraction was the conclusion she reached, even if it didn't account for everything. It didn't explain why the tender moments *before* their first kiss were dominant in her mind. It didn't justify how spectacular everything in the back seat of his car had been.

She told herself that she hadn't fallen in love. Or if she had, not enough to change her plans. The possibility that she might have fallen just a little bit kept nibbling at her. Cash was proving harder to forget than she had hoped.

There was no forgetting the possibility of reopening the Moonglow, however, now that she'd mentioned it to her family. They wouldn't *let* her forget it. After two days of nonstop family pressure, she caved in and called the first drive-in for information.

After that, she began working mornings at the deli and spending afternoons and evenings visiting drive-ins. It kept her busy—and made her increasingly interested.

Learning from chats with owners and operators that business was brisk and booming in the right locations, she turned to investigating how much it would cost to get the Moonglow up and running for a year.

After a week of investigations, she had decided what—and what not—to do with herself during the year ahead. With her insurance money in the bank and a business plan on paper, she sat down with her family and told them she'd be sleeping on the couch and helping in the deli no more.

They were thrilled.

"Are we invited to Weston for the grand opening?" Larry wanted to know.

"Of course. If you can break away from the deli."

"We'll close shop for a day or so," Linda said. "What's your first main feature going to be?"

"Guess."

Her father clapped his hands. "*Wild West?*"

"What else?" Larinda confirmed. "If you can both come down for the opening, I'll feature you in my advertising."

"I can see the ad now," said Larry with a dramatic wave of his hand. "'Meet actual actors from the movie! Get their autographs before showtime!'"

"'The two, the *only* Larry and Linda Outlaw!'" Linda chimed in.

Larinda exchanged an indulgent grin with Larson. "Do you want in on the publicity, too, Brother?"

"Sure, if I'm around."

"Why wouldn't you be around?"

"Because I joined up with the U.S. Army today. I'll be leaving for boot camp in a month or so."

Like her parents, Larinda didn't know whether to cheer or cry. Larson had been wanting to be a soldier since he was eight years old. Now, at eighteen, he'd grown old enough.

"My baby brother a soldier?"

"Best damn recruit an army could have," he confirmed with a snappy salute. "When does the Moonglow have its big night?"

"Before you leave, Larson." Larinda crossed her fingers for luck. "If everything goes according to plan."

9

CASH WAS TORN between smiling and scowling at the plain postcard he received three weeks after Larinda's departure from Weston.

"I'll return on Thursday," it read, "to live and work until I sell the Moonglow. Larinda Outlaw."

She'd be back tomorrow, would she? Two days before April Fool's day. He felt giddy one moment, glum the next, as he reread each word of Larinda's terse notice. He'd missed her too much not to feel joyful at the prospect of seeing her again. She'd be back! He'd missed her too much not to be disturbed by the intensity of those feelings. She'd be back....

Now he was stuck between a rock and a hard place again. There was no mistaking the tone of that single curt sentence. She hadn't begun the card "Dear Cash." She hadn't written one warm, friendly word. She hadn't signed off "Looking forward to seeing you."

In tone and content, what she had written made clear that there would be no homey dinners after work. No oatmeal chewies in the cookie jar. No back-seat reunions at the drive-in.

He should be happy. He wasn't.

"WANNA GO bowling?" Dan asked that night after a dinner of canned vegetable soup and peanut-butter sandwiches.

"Not tonight, Scout."

"Gee, you never wanna go anymore. Ever since Larinda left."

"She's coming back. Tomorrow."

"Wow! Yippee! Oatmeal chewies again!"

Cash shook his head. "She's just coming to live next door and work in town until next year. It won't be like it was before."

Dan's face fell. "Not like a family?"

"We're family enough for each other, Dan."

"Aren't you ever gonna marry Larinda, Dad?"

"No. She's not my type."

"She's *my* type," Dan persisted. "Just the kinda Mom I want. She didn't look icky when I showed her my bugs."

"Show Larinda your garter snake tomorrow and watch her look icky."

"Bet she'll like it."

"Bet she won't."

"What's your type, Dad?"

Not red hair and brown eyes. "Let's go bowling, Dan."

THE FLEA MARKET was teeming when Larinda returned Thursday afternoon. She pulled her car, packed with bargain-basement household items and clothes, around to her trailer. She had scheduled her arrival so that Cash would be busy with the market and Dan not home yet from school. By the time she had to face either of them, she'd be moved in and unpacked.

She found a happy-face "welcome back" drawing from Dan taped to her front door. Nothing from Cash, however. Not that she had counted on anything. Indeed, welcome was the last thing she expected from him. It would get even worse once he found out what she intended to do.

She had already planned how, when and where she'd tell him. Until then she would get settled—and gird for battle.

Dan played right into her plan when he got home from school and found her unloading the last box from her car. He ran to tell Cash where he'd be, then rushed back to inform her of everything that had happened in her absence. He spent the afternoon helping her clean and unpack. From him Larinda learned that Cash had gone out on four dates with four different women while she'd been gone.

"He didn't like any of them," Dan said. "He told Walt they were a waste of time and money. I heard."

"You shouldn't repeat what you hear," she gently reproved.

Cash dating? What had prompted it? And why had her heart plummeted at the news? More disturbing was why her heart now soared at the knowledge that Cash felt they were a waste.

"Was your dad busy when you last saw him, Dan?"

"Yeah. Holed up in his office doing paperwork."

"Let's take a walk through the market, then. I need to stretch my legs after my long drive."

She went out with Dan and merged into the crowd with him. He hung on to her hand when she stopped to chat with Annie first, then Mrs. Soames.

"Looks like someone missed someone a lot," Mrs. Soames said to her after a glance at Dan. "The man in charge around here missed someone, too, I'm thinking."

"Not a chance of that," Larinda replied. "He was glad to see me gone."

Mrs. Soames raised her eyebrows and focused over Larinda's shoulder. "I'd say he's glad to see you back right now. Here he comes, hiding a smile."

Larinda turned and saw Cash moving through the crowd. She couldn't detect that he was hiding even the remotest smile. Mrs. Soames had to be seeing wrong, for he was approaching, looking distinctly unhappy that she had returned.

"Have a good drive up?" he stiffly inquired when he reached them.

"Not bad," Larinda replied, keeping her eyes on his shoes. The rest of him was too good to look at after not seeing him for three weeks.

"Dan's been a big help with my unpacking," she said, lifting her focus as far as Cash's knees. It was a crime for a man to look so virile and masculine from the soles of his shoes up. "I'll have to pay him back somehow."

Dan grinned. "Pay me with oatmeal chewies."

"How about with pizza tonight?" Larinda suggested, skipping Cash's erogenous zone to focus on his middle shirt button before adding, "for the three of us."

"I don't think—" Cash began.

"Yippee! Pizza, Dad. Please?"

"I have *you* to thank, too, for letting Dan help," Larinda said to prompt Cash out of his obvious reluctance.

Her plan was that Dan would play the video games at the pizza parlor while she broke her news to Cash. It was safer to do it in a public place. He wouldn't make a scene there as she was sure he would in private. He wouldn't strangle her in front of his son and the good people of Weston.

Cash would have to be restrained and businesslike about it at Weston's most crowded and popular pizza parlor. He'd have to take the news sitting down and remain seated.

Cash frowned. "Dan—"

"Please with chocolate syrup and whipped cream on top, Dad?"

Larinda glanced higher and saw Cash looking at her. She managed a casual rise of her eyebrows and a noncommittal shrug. "I'll drive, too," she offered. That way, he'd have to hear her out or walk the ten miles back to the Moonglow. "My treat all around."

"Yeah, Dad. No sweat."

Cash finally said, "Pizza sounds decent enough."

She began backing away. "I have more unpacking to do in the meantime."

"I'll help some more," Dan said, clinging to her hand.

She feasted her eyes on Cash for a moment as he turned and walked away. Then she directed them firmly away from him—and away from Mrs. Soames's knowing smile.

Strolling back in the direction of the trailer with Dan, Larinda buoyed herself with the hope that her announcement would prompt Cash to take her up on her original offer. She wouldn't mind that happening at all. If it did, she'd stay only long enough to sell the Moonglow. If it didn't, she'd show movies against his every objection.

Nothing, not a hurricane or a quirk in a will or Cash Bowman, would keep her from being self-employed and self-sufficient.

"YOU PLAN to *what?*" Cash stared at Larinda over the last piece of pizza, aware that several heads in the place swiveled his way at the rise in his voice.

"You heard me," Larinda murmured. "And everyone has certainly heard *you*. Pipe down."

"Movies," he growled, glaring at her. "A fool idea if I ever heard one."

Larinda shook her head. "A very sound idea, as the theater operators I talked to recently can testify. Those in the right locations are doing quite well as drive-ins by night and flea markets by day. I intend to do this for a year. I'll see a much better return on my investment this way than if I banked my nest egg and worked a nickel-and-dime job here in Weston."

"I'll have to close earlier than I do now," he retorted, his unblinking eyes focused squarely on her. "Closing earlier means reduced profits for me from the concession stand. It means reduced sales for every seller at the market. The close of every market day will be a monumental scramble for me and my cleanup people."

"The flea-market operators I talked with did have their part to do," Larinda said with a nod of agreement.

"You know good and well I'm no movie fan, Larinda. What do I want with movies showing in my front yard all night?"

"No one is forcing you to live on the property, Cash."

"It's harassment pure and simple," he hotly accused. "You're trying to force me out."

Heads turned again. Larinda smiled for effect and made her voice deliberately low. "I'm trying to coexist, unless you feel more like selling out now than you did before." She raised her eyebrows. "If so, my offer still stands."

"I already told you what you can do with your offer—and your movies."

"That leaves coexistence, then. You do your part and I'll do mine and we'll both profit."

"You won't profit if no one comes to your passion pit."

"Since the closest one is a hundred miles from Weston, I believe they'll come to mine from miles around. My only competition is Weston's existing indoor theaters and I doubt they'll be lowering their admission price to beat mine."

"Don't think everyone in Weston will be thrilled to hear you plan to show movies, Red. A drive-in isn't a big plus in a family neighborhood like Cleve Davis intends that parcel of his to be."

"He hasn't broken ground yet," Larinda pointed out. "By the time he gets his houses under construction, I'll have sold the Moonglow—probably to Davis himself."

Cash shook his head. "He's moving faster than that on his plans. When he gets wind of this, you'll find yourself arguing the issue at next week's town council meeting."

"I expect I'll have to argue it anyway. The theater operators I've talked to told me to anticipate opposition from certain local groups."

Cash sat back in his chair, his expression changing from furious to ominous. Wary of the shift in his mood, Larinda sat back, too.

"Land values could nose-dive by the time you sell," he said. "Davis has had financial ups and downs before now. He could be in a down cycle or bankrupt when you go to market for land value. What then?"

"I'll have a thriving drive-in to sell, in that case."

"Not if 'certain local groups' and Davis's prospective home buyers mount a successful opposition."

"Negative thinking isn't my style, Cash."

"Or mine, either, Red. I just happen to want to buy one of the houses he's going to build out there. As a future homeowner, why shouldn't I be concerned about the quality of my neighborhood? Everyone else who wants to buy out there will be concerned, as well."

His tone had become too quiet, she thought. There was calculation in it now. He looked as if he'd begun hatching a plan she couldn't intuit.

To prevent him from thinking he could thwart her, she said, "All the theater operators I talked to had to overcome local opposition. I'll proceed exactly as they did. If I have to present my plan to the town council when it meets again next week, I'll be ready for the naysayers."

Cash drained his beer mug in one long gulp and wiped his mouth on his sleeve. "I'll be there to say nay."

LARINDA DIDN'T let Cash or his threats stop her from applying for every necessary business license and permit in the next few days. She busily secured bids for the screen and sound-system repairs and looked into local advertising costs. During that time, as Cash had predicted, she was informed that she'd have to present her plan at next week's council meeting before her permit could be approved and issued.

Between arranging for repairs and preparing for the meeting, she saw only glimpses of Cash as he left or entered his trailer. She saw more of Dan, who dropped in and out over the weekend and during the first half of the following week. His visits were welcome tension relievers as Wednesday, the night of the town meeting, approached.

His eyes were so like Cash's. She never gazed into them without a pang in her heart. She experienced one of those jolts during Dan's drop-in on Wednesday afternoon as she was preparing for the meeting to come. As she looked into his eyes, she reflected that if things had been different from the start, she and Cash might have been on friendly terms—or even falling in love—right now instead of bracing for war. War it would be tonight at the town council meeting.

Word had spread fast of the plan she would be presenting. She'd had only to tell Walt of what she intended to do, before her phone rang with a call from his wife's friend, Eva Maycomb.

Eva, Weston's leading preservationist and town historian, had welcomed Larinda's news and proceeded to explain that she, the Historical Society and many Weston citizens were opposed to the urban sprawl that developers like Cleve Davis produced.

A diehard no-growth advocate, Eva had pledged the society's support for the Moonglow to be refurbished if it became an issue. "That drive-in will be a cultural and historical asset to the community," she had asserted. "It's pure Americana, it is."

Larinda had hastened to say that she intended to sell the Moonglow, Americana or not, in a year for land value or business value, whichever was greater.

"No matter," Eva had responded. "Every no-growth advocate in Weston wants to see Davis Development's plans blocked. If this will make Cleve give up and build in some other town, we'll achieve our primary aim. Everything else is secondary."

"That doesn't change my intent to sell to Davis—or anyone else who wants to buy—next year," Larinda continued to remind her, puzzled by the society's evident lack of logic. "What happens if I sell to a land developer?"

"You won't," said Eva. "We've already consulted with Mrs. Soames on that. She says you won't sell—not for land value."

"I most certainly will," Larinda protested. "I can't accept the society's support on that basis. Furthermore, if Davis gives up and builds elsewhere, I might be out of a buyer when I'm able to sell."

"You'll be out of business *now* if you let him block you, young lady. Is that what you want?"

"Of course not, but—"

"Only the good Lord—and Mrs. Soames—knows what we'll all be facing in a year," Eva had cut in. "We can't be worrying that far into the future before we worry about right now, can we?"

Unable to summon any compelling argument, Larinda had made an appointment to meet early in the week with Eva and several of her no-growth sympathizers to acquaint them with her plan. She had talked to Eva again this morning.

"Every believer in no growth will be at the meeting to support you," Eva had assured. "I've enlisted them all to speak on your behalf. Cleve Davis doesn't want that theater operating, but we do if it will prevent him from suburbanizing Weston. By the way, I hear Chester's son is joining forces with him."

That unwelcome news had kept Larinda tense right up to the night of the meeting.

On Wednesday night, her fingers fumbled and shook as she got dressed for the council meeting. She hoped they wouldn't shake when she addressed the council. Would Cash speak on Davis's behalf as Eva would speak on hers? If so, what would he have to say?

She was still speculating when she drove out of the Moonglow alone that evening. Cash had left only moments before she did. She saw a strange car parked in front of his trailer—Dan's sitter for the night, no doubt. Walt waved her out with his flashlight.

The meeting was already packed when she walked in. She spotted Cash, in a business suit, talking on one side of the hall to a big, burly man who had to be Cleve Davis. He looked born to bulldoze raw land into shopping malls and housing developments.

Around him and Cash stood more men in business suits. Davis's investors, Larinda surmised. She was glad she had stretched her budget and bought a business suit of her own for the occasion.

On the opposite side of the hall she spied out Eva Maycomb and her troops. Larinda saw that Eva looked as straitlaced and earnestly righteous tonight as she'd looked that first day at the flea market. The young woman standing next to her bore a strong resemblance to Eva. Her daughter, Larinda decided. Probably the one who had first informed Fran Whitman that Cash slept alone.

She wondered if Eva's daughter had been one of Cash's four dates. It shouldn't have made her feel good that he hadn't enjoyed his night out with such a comely young blonde. It shouldn't have, but it did.

She stole a second glance at Cash on her way to join Eva, and caught him watching her. *Get used to it*, she told herself. *He'll be staring daggers when you stand up to speak.* Daggers weren't in his stare at that moment, though. It was desire that she read in it right then. Raw, rampant desire.

She looked away. *Damn him.* He'd done that to unnerve her. She shouldn't have even glanced his way. And she shouldn't have been so struck at how handsome he looked in a suit and tie. She headed straight for Eva.

Cash watched Larinda join Eva's group. *Damn her.* She'd caught him ogling her and shot back a sexy look to throw him off. He hadn't been able to help it. Though she was dressed for business, all he'd thought about was bed when he first caught sight of her. Her legs seemed twice as long in hose and high heels, her hair twice as red against the charcoal gray of her suit.

"Hey-hey-hey," Cleve Davis said after following Cash's darting glance. "Is that tasty morsel married or on the loose?"

"Single," Cash muttered, stifling an urge to punch Davis out right then and there.

"Wow." Davis's chief investor lowered his horn-rim glasses and gazed out over them at Larinda. "Double wow. Triple—"

"Don't wow the opposition," Cash cut in, balling his fists in his pants pockets. "She's why we're here."

Another investor held an imaginary pair of binoculars to his eyes. "*That's* Outlaw?"

"In person." Cash shifted from foot to foot, restraining the urge to land a right hook on more than one nose. Why hadn't she come in a burlap granny dress? Why hadn't she worn her hair in a sexless bun like Eva's, instead of loose and waving down her back?

If she had, he wouldn't be grinding his teeth against everything he felt like saying. Like *Want your lights put out, wolfman?* Or *Eyes off, hands off, she's mine.*

"So she's what answered your phone that day I called," Davis said to Cash with a slow smile. "Kidsitting, was she?"

"Dan was sick. Flu bug. She was . . . convenient."

"How convenient is she otherwise, pal?" Davis winked. "I could make myself sleep with *that* enemy."

Cash might have decked him if Barbi Davis hadn't walked up right then and taken her husband's arm. Cash couldn't decide which of them he disliked most at that moment, Cleve for leering at Larinda or Barbi for reminding him of Rita. She had Rita's roving eye, one Cash had felt rove over his body one too many times in the fifteen minutes he'd known her. If Davis had the instincts of a tomcat, his wife was the female counterpart.

Seeing the council members filing in, Cash took a seat—next to Cleve, not Barbi. A glance back at everyone else getting seated showed the hall split down the middle between Davis's and Larinda's supporters.

The meeting got under way, with parliamentary rigmarole and routine council matters to be dispensed with before the Moonglow came up for discussion. The instant it did, the restless audience stilled and leaned forward.

Larinda was the first to speak. Calm and succinct, she began by describing the renaissance of drive-in theaters around the country: Asheville, Tennessee; Fayetteville, Arkansas; Durham, North Carolina; Commerce, Georgia; San Jose, California. She went on to outline her own plan for the Moonglow and cited her projections regarding traffic volume and the probable need for a four-way stop at the main intersection to the theater. She ended by citing every possible positive aspect of a refurbished Moonglow operating in Weston.

Cleve Davis, when he spoke next, listed every possible negative associated with a drive-in theater in a neighborhood setting: noise, traffic, lights. His craggy voice described the subdivision he intended to build as "family oriented" and charged that drive-ins in such settings interfered with the quality of family life.

Hearing that, Larinda wished she had stressed the fact that baby boomers and their families formed the core of every successful drive-in's enthusiastic audience. The theaters she had visited in the L.A. area had been attended in large numbers by parents with small children in tow. She made a note for Eva to stress the fact for her.

Eva spoke after Cleve. "Drive-ins," she contended, "are as American as Big Macs, baseball and the Liberty Bell. They're not only entertainment American-style, they're *family* entertainment. The history of this country is disappearing right before our eyes," she further contended. "Drive-ins are an endangered species of American history and I say let's give the one we have a chance to survive."

Cash spoke after Eva. "Ever heard the term 'passion pit'?" he inquired of the council. "I don't know about you, but I don't want one in *my* back yard. I don't want X-rated movies showing on a screen my child can see from any window in the house I buy, either."

Larinda seethed. Here was a true stab in the back. He knew she'd never show X-rated movies, yet he had run up that red flag without a second thought for her integrity. If anything, *he* was the one who'd helped the term 'passion pit' flourish in his teenage years.

"I was that kind of boy," she remembered him saying. *The nerve.* Any remaining trust she might have had in his integrity was obliterated now. He was capable of anything. Anything.

As the meeting progressed, every spokesperson for every conceivable cause made an opinion known. Environmental activists spoke out against the loss of open space. Church leaders voiced their concerns about a drive-in's contribution to the delinquency of minors. Like Cash, potential buyers of Davis's homes objected to the Moonglow operating at night.

At meeting's end, the council appointed a citizens' committee to study the question of use of the area and instructed them to report their findings at the end of two weeks. Larinda was requested to halt the drive-in repairs during that time.

Two weeks, she despaired, after driving home from the meeting. With repairs halted, what was she going to do with herself for all of that time? *Preview old movies*, she decided after a doleful glance at her new VCR. She couldn't afford to rent and watch movies full-time, however.

What else? *Wallpaper my bedroom.* Yes, she'd do that with the most romantic floral wallpaper available at a bargain price in Weston. The next fourteen days promised to be difficult to fill if she wouldn't be busy overseeing repairs. They'd also be lonely with no friendly neighbor besides Dan. Having romance on her walls would compensate for the utter lack of it in her life.

What else? *Plant a garden.* If Cash had any hope that she'd give up and go home in the face of his and Davis's opposition, he could forget it. A nice, big vegetable garden behind her trailer would let him know she intended to stay and fight with every intention of winning.

10

CASH AWOKE EARLIER than usual the morning after the council meeting. He lay watching dawn filter through his bedroom window, remembering the look on Larinda's face after he'd made his inflammatory comment to the council. The X-rated-movie attack had been Cleve's brainchild.

"You have a kid," he'd told Cash. "I don't. That line of complaint should come from a daddy like you."

As much as it had to be said, Cash still had a sour feeling in his stomach from voicing it. He didn't think for a minute that Larinda would sully the Moonglow's screen with porno movies. It had happened, though, in other communities. Davis's investors had done enough research on the issue to know.

Larinda had looked not only furious but betrayed. Considering his personal history with her to date, he shouldn't care how she had looked. Rather, he should care what the effect of her plan would be on him if she put it into action. Closing early. Reduced profits. Movies all night.

He shouldn't feel underhanded for being the first to tip Davis off to Larinda's plan so Cleve could fight it at city hall. Someone else would have put that bug in Cleve's ear, now wouldn't they have? You bet. And why feel guilty about stalling her plan, when she wasn't racked with self-reproach about cutting into the flea-market's profits?

Yet he felt guilty as all get out.

He raked his fingers through his hair and eased out of bed. Every morning since Larinda's return he'd awakened with a superhuman erection. Today was no different.

It was good to feel virile, he reflected, good to feel strong and potent. He enjoyed feeling sexually healthy and thoroughly male. But *this* virile? *This* strong and potent? All because of the redhead next door?

She occupied his mind through his shower, through his first cup of coffee, through his rush to get Dan ready for school. She was still firmly entrenched in his thoughts when he hurried out to open the market for the day.

Later that morning, he was thinking so hard about her that he walked smack into her during a stroll he was taking through the market crowd.

"Watch where you're going," she said, scowling, hopping on one foot because he'd accidentally stepped on the other.

"Sorry. I didn't see you."

She limped around in a circle to ease her trod-on toes into action again. "Hair this red isn't hard to miss, Cash."

"I said I was sorry." He scowled back at her, eyeing the DOWN WITH DAVIS! UP WITH MOONGLOW! lapel pin she wore. "What are you doing out here? Drumming up support for your side at *my* market?"

"That and shopping for a shovel and a hoe." She limped two yards to a hardware-vendor's stand.

Cash followed. "A shovel and hoe for what?"

"For the garden I intend to plant today behind my trailer."

"Two nice spades here," the vendor told her, pointing out the best of his used gardening implements. "Not too rusty. And that slant-hoe next to them is still pretty sharp."

Larinda examined the tools, refusing to look at Cash. Couldn't stand him. Damned if she'd lay even one eye on him after his stab in the back last night. X-rated movies, indeed. Of all the negative things that would stick in people's minds, that comment would top the list.

"What do you need a garden for?" she heard Cash growl behind her.

Although she didn't owe him a reply, she forced one out. "I want fresh green salad, that's why. And summer squash, not to mention a watermelon a week if I can get enough to grow."

"After last night, I wouldn't plan to be here come summer if I were you," he advised.

Larinda said to the vendor, "I'll take this hoe and this shovel." Glancing over her shoulder at Cash, she said, "If I were you, I'd plan to hire twice the market cleanup help you have now. You'll need to get the job done in half the time when I open this place for movies."

"Only if Davis loses out at city hall," Cash retorted walking away.

"I'm betting he will," Larinda called after him.

He muttered something she couldn't make out and disappeared into the crowd. He was a master at ruining a perfectly nice morning, she thought. She looked to the vendor for moral support and got it, to her surprise.

He grinned and pulled a lapel pin identical to hers from his shirt pocket. "I take it off when I see Cash coming," he said. "Soon as he passes, I put it back on. I wear this other one with it." He fished out a second pin, which advertised JOE BOB BRIGGS FOR PRESIDENT.

Readily recognizing the name of the nation's best-known drive-in movie critic, Larinda laughed with glee. "You," she said, "are a true subversive—and a very welcome ally."

He laughed, too. "I read Joe Bob's column every week. I'm not the only one around here, either. Joe Bob's fans are all rootin' for you. We'd like to see all those classic drive-in movies he writes about."

"You will," Larinda promised him, handing over the price of the shovel and hoe.

She walked away with her purchase, happy about the vendor's support. There was a twinge, however, when she thought of how she'd advised Cash to hire more help. Well, he *would* need it. So why reproach herself over the complications her plan would cause Cash? She had as much right to make a living as he did. If her operation would cut into his profits slightly, that was show biz. She had problems, as well. Because of the market, she wouldn't be opening the theater for movies as early as she'd like.

Too, she had to suspect Cash of being first to notify Cleve Davis of her intentions. That strong suspicion was reason enough to assuage any reason for self-reproach.

Furthermore, had he felt even a pang of regret at turning down her buy-out offer? No. Well, maybe he'd felt something. He *had* come over that first morning with champagne and roses, but only because he'd felt sorry for her. He wasn't feeling one iota as guilty as she did now, she was sure.

Making her way to another vendor's stand, she bought garden seeds. When Cash saw the garden going in, he'd get the message that she intended to be in business at harvest time.

Fueled by determination, guilt, anger and a good measure of sexual frustration, she worked the soil behind her trailer for several hours with her new tools. Dan joined her when he got home from school.

"What are you doing with yourself this afternoon?" she asked him.

"Going on my extraspecial nature walk. Want to go?"

Larinda leaned on her hoe and surveyed the large patch of ground she'd weeded and tilled. "Yes. A walk in the fields would be nice."

They headed off together on a tramp through the fields. There, Dan showed Larinda where he'd found Gertie the garter snake, and where a trap-door spider lay in wait for unsuspecting insects. He pointed out rabbit holes and weasel tracks. Near a large grove of cottonwood trees, he whispered that a pair of foxes had a den there.

Larinda returned from her nature walk with more love than ever in her heart for Daniel Eric Bowman. It wasn't wise to love Cash's son so much, but her heart couldn't help it.

THE DAY BEFORE the council meeting Larinda had most of the ingredients for tossed salad sprouting in her garden. She'd also wallpapered her bedroom and had previewed as many movies as she could afford to rent.

In that time, there had been more afternoon rambles in the fields with Dan, and two days spent with Eva and Mrs. Soames making more of the DOWN WITH DAVIS! UP WITH MOONGLOW! lapel pins. At one pin-making session, Eva had confided that Cash had dated her daughter just once recently, confirming Larinda's hunch that she had been one of the four Dan had mentioned.

"He didn't try for as much as a good-night kiss, she says," Eva had sniffed. "He doesn't prefer blondes, it seems."

Larinda had been hard-pressed not to look relieved. She thought she had succeeded until she caught Mrs. Soames smiling wisely at her over the piles of lapel pins.

Now as Larinda got ready for bed the night before the special council meeting, she recalled that wise smile. She also remembered the prediction Mrs. Soames had made the morning she'd taken care of Dan:

You won't be away from here long after you leave . . . you're going to bide by that motherless boy—and his, lonesome dad—longer than you think.

It had turned out true enough to make a person believe in second sight and the existence of the spiritual ozone, Larinda mused. It didn't make her believe she'd never sell the Moonglow, however. After pulling on the big T-shirt she wore for sleep, she got into bed and turned out her lamp.

Larinda closed her eyes, still seeing Mrs. Soames's smile. Though unspoken, the comment across the table had been, *You care quite a bit for Cash Bowman. I see how much it pleases you to hear he didn't kiss Connie Maycomb good-night.*

Larinda felt pleased again now at the recollection. After two weeks of lonely nights and semi-lonely days, she couldn't deny caring quite a bit for Cash despite the many reasons she had not to care for him at all.

There was more to it than that, of course. She had gotten more than sexually involved with him during her initial stay and couldn't forget how right she had felt being in his home, sharing his table, caring for his son. As for how right she had felt in the back seat of his Chevy, it was impossible to forget.

Every night she went to sleep longing for his arms around her. Every night she took meager comfort in the knowledge that he wasn't out dating. The Chevy hadn't left the carport any evening since her return, except for the council meeting. He'd stayed home each night, as she had. And tonight Dan was staying over at Jeffie's. Cash was alone.

She pictured herself slipping into Cash's trailer, into his bed, into the passion and tenderness of his embrace. Did he picture himself like that with her, too? Unable to resist? Unable to sleep one more night in solitude?

Alone. Alone.

LARINDA AWOKE in the dark to the keen of rising wind and the gritty rumble of thunder overhead. *Hurricane!* She jerked up from her pillow and heard the drum of rain on the trailer roof. *Oh, God. Oh, God.*

Crashing waves of wind and water would smash, twist and sweep everything away. Trees, homes, entire city blocks gone. Everything ripped out from the roots. Nothing left. Just rubble. Ruin. Devastation. Death.

Wild-eyed, with shrieks rising in her throat, she bolted out of bed. *Cash.* She had to get to him. He'd made it stop before. He'd stop it now. *Cash.*

She burst through the front door of her trailer. Wind-driven rain lashed her face, plastered her hair and T-shirt to her body. It was dark. She could see nothing. Mud oozed between her bare toes. She slipped, slid, and lost her footing.

"Cash!" she screamed, reaching into the blinding storm. "Help!"

"Red!"

She felt his hand first, gripping her and, pulling her up. Then one arm slid under her shoulders and the other hooked under her knees. He lifted her, his bare chest heaving against her cheek. Oh, Cash.

"I'm here. Right here." He held her to him protectively under the downpour. He felt her cling to him, shivering in the cradle of his arms.

She had been his first thought when he'd woken to the growl of thunder. Nothing had mattered but reaching her, sheltering her from fear.

He carried her back into her trailer and elbowed a light switch on. Sinking into the nearest chair, he rocked her in his arms and stroked her streaming hair.

He pressed his lips to her wet forehead. She had called to him, run to him, needed him. It made him feel like a hero.

She was still shivering from the rain and shaking with fear. She needed more warmth than his bare chest and soaked briefs could provide. He rose and carried her to the bathroom. A loud crack overhead tightened her clasp around his neck and brought a stricken sound from her throat.

"Sshh. I'm with you, Red. Nothing bad can happen." He kneed the seat down on the toilet and set her on it. Framing her pale face in his hands, he inquired, "How does a nice, warm shower sound?"

Larinda could only nod and tremble. Though slightly calmer now, she couldn't yet trust that a scream wouldn't squeeze past any word if she spoke. She wasn't rational enough yet to feel modest or shy when he stripped off her sodden T-shirt. It didn't even quite register that he was wearing wet briefs and nothing else. She touched his hip just to maintain the security of contact when he leaned away to turn on the shower tap.

"Too bad these trailers don't have bathtubs," he muttered, adjusting the water temperature. He drew the curtain aside and turned back to her. "There. Just right. Step in."

Helped by his hands curled around hers, unsure that her shaking knees would hold her, she slowly rose, and swayed on her feet.

Cash wasn't feeling all that stable himself. He was almost nude in a tiny bathroom with a nude woman. He had stripped her shirt off expecting panties underneath and found none. She stood before him now, a true redhead in every respect, gorgeous to behold. *And scared to death,* he reminded himself.

"Right this way," he prompted, steering her toward the warm spray.

"Ah," she gasped when it hit her skin.

Cash hadn't intended to follow Larinda in, briefs and all, but it happened that way. Maybe because he was as chilled as she, and his feet just as muddy. Maybe because she looked unsteady on her own. Maybe because he had been apart from her too long and couldn't bear the slightest distance now.

Whatever the reason, he stood behind her in the shower, cupping her shoulders. Steam swirled around him. He closed his eyes and made himself think of cold things and places rather than Larinda's warming flesh or the curve of her bottom against his bare thighs. He pictured snow five feet deep rather than her raspberry-tipped breasts just a touch away and the fiery triangle of hair he had possessed but not clearly seen until tonight.

In time he felt Larinda turn around. He knew not to open his eyes with her facing him. "Better?" he whispered.

"Yes." She laced her fingers with his, no longer shaking now, no longer stiff and speechless with fright. "Thank you. Again."

"Warm enough?"

"Quite. And you?"

"Yeah." Any warmer, an inch closer and he'd be on the rise.

"Cash, would you . . . stay with me tonight?"

"Stay?" He opened his eyes and met hers. They were dark in her face, serious, searching and vulnerable.

She nodded. "Please?"

His body answered before his mouth did. He struggled to stop the rise in his soaked briefs. The need in Larinda's eyes thawed his control in an instant.

"Yes." If she needed him through this storm-tossed night, he needed her just as badly. How could he sleep in his own bed knowing she was alone and terrified in hers? How could he sleep with his body aching for her as it ached now?

"You will?"

He didn't repeat himself to assure her that he meant what he'd said. He held her face up to his kiss and she came against him in one fluid move under the spray, all his to hold and taste and touch.

Sweeping Larinda up again, dripping wet, Cash carried her to her bed and covered her body with his. Flashes of lightning lit the room, but it wasn't the storm that made Larinda whimper and cry out now. It was Cash's mouth sliding over her water-slick breasts and sucking the moisture from her nipples. It was each muscle and contour of his body under her fingers when she slid his briefs down. Then it was his rigid flesh, hard and smooth in her stroking hands.

"Red..." He lay back and touched her wrist. "Stop..."

"Let me, Cash. Without condoms we can't have it all. So let me."

He couldn't argue with her. Her sensuous stroke and the enchantment of her mouth made any protest impossible. A man on his back at the mercy of a passionate, generous woman could poise at the brink only so long. He plunged over with a low, unraveling groan.

Larinda laid her cheek on his chest and listened to the beat of his heart slow. She traced her fingers through his chest hair to his nipples. Hard as pebbles before, they were softer now, less defined.

"Red. What have you done to me?"

"Pleased you, I hope."

"Words fail me," he confirmed, holding her close. He touched her breast, groaned again, then shifted and pressed her onto her back. "I'll make them fail you, too."

She fell into silent rapture as Cash kissed her mouth with tongue-thrusting depth and made a lavish feast of her breasts.

She opened to the slipping, sliding, intimate touch of his fingers—and then his mouth between her thighs. He plunged his tongue deeply into her and kept it moving. Over and over he courted her response.

Spread open to Cash and writhing in passion, Larinda had no awareness of the storm outside. She knew only that everything he was doing made her feel as she'd never felt before. She felt special, unique, beautiful. How could she not? He was telling her so with dark murmurs and soft, sucking kisses in the delicate folds of her sex.

She arched up to the press of his lips, the supple stroke of his tongue.

"Timberrrr," she whispered, as her body shuddered with pleasure.

CASH WAS GONE when Larinda awoke the next morning. He'd gone? Without a word or a last kiss? Yes. She knew men well enough to know what that meant. It never meant anything good.

The sun was high in a cloudless sky, beaming too cheerily through the curtains. She flopped back onto her pillow. It smelled of Cash. Everything smelled of him, her skin, her hair, the sheets, the air. As she gazed around at the flowered walls of her bedroom, a rush of tears filled her eyes.

Dear God, she had not only slept with the enemy, she *loved* him. Thunder, lightning, wind, rain, panic and fear had all conspired to make it so. Nothing would undo it. She had the feeling now that she'd been in love with Cash Bowman from the first day.

What had started it? She thought back. That bare chest of his across the desk? The blue flecks in his gray eyes? The way he cupped his hand to Dan's little head that day? The champagne and roses? Heaven only knew.

She smudged her tears on her cheeks with a handful of hair. *In love.* With a man who didn't know movies from Rototillers. A man who wasn't the least bit blond.

A man who had made love more than once last night, twice with the lights on. He had run next door for condoms as promised. Everything had been possible then. Little had gone unexplored.

What a lover he had been! What an adversary he remained!

What had she done? She'd have to face him at the council meeting tonight. Her entire body blushed at the thought. Where had reasonable thoughts like that hidden themselves last night? Not in the shower. Not in the bed.

Clever of them to crop up now, too late to make a woman think better of loving a man. One last word this morning, one touch, one farewell kiss would have left her feeling less foolish now. *Fool.*

CASH SAT in his third class of the day, as dazed as if he'd been struck by lightning the night before. *Love.* He didn't have room for it. Or time for it. Or any reason on earth to feel it for Larinda Outlaw.

Why hadn't he remembered that last night? The run he'd made to his trailer had been so fleet he'd barely gotten damp in the torrential rain. A matter of seconds and he'd been back in Larinda's bed, loving her.

The only thing he hadn't done after that was say "I love you." She hadn't said it, either, thank God. Because she hadn't felt it? A hateful thought.

But he should love that thought. He'd make damn sure he believed it, too, before he faced her tonight in front of the council. Last night, he'd forgotten about the meeting tonight. All night long he'd forgotten. Only this morning had he remembered and escaped before he could forget again. Once a fool, twice a fool. No thirds for him.

11

LARINDA DROVE into Weston before Cash and Dan got home from school. Her timing was deliberate. After last night, facing Cash would be more than her emotions could handle.

She put her suit and heels in the car to change into for the council meeting, then drove to the multiplex in Weston's biggest shopping mall to watch movies all day. It had four mini-theaters with one movie each, enough to last up to meeting time. None of the four features looked romantic. Her lucky day.

She started with a suspense thriller and followed that with a science-fantasy adventure. Only two kisses and some brief nudity in the first film made her think of Cash. Next came a horror flick. There was no romance in that one to distract her.

Last came a murder mystery. It was steamy, sexy and erotic in the first half, just what she didn't need. The true mystery was how she could be aroused by every pant and sigh on the screen. Luckily, one of the lovers got murdered around halfway through, so the rest provided no further reminders of the night she'd spent.

Movied out, Larinda changed clothes in the mall rest room and drove to the meeting. The scene at city hall was much the same as it had been two weeks earlier. Cash wore the same suit and kept his back to the no-growth half of the hall. Over his shoulder, she saw

Cleve Davis send a broad, bawdy wink her way. She iced him with a yawn.

Eva had her son, Garner, instead of her daughter with her this time. Larinda realized why when Eva gushed slightly in introducing him to her. He was as attractive and blond as Connie and equally available, she surmised from Eva's eager manner. Back in her love-those-blondes days, Larinda would have welcomed the introduction. A surreptitious glance at Cash told her she'd be smart to welcome it now.

His attitude was clear by the stonewall stance he had taken. She told herself it was only to be expected. He hadn't done the asking last night, after all. She'd done it on her own. He had come running in the storm, yes, but then raced back in the opposite direction when it was all over.

She was old enough to accept that a man couldn't be blamed for taking up an offer from a naked woman in a shower. She'd made it with no strings attached; he'd taken it the same way. That had been best for them both—hadn't it?—for someone stood to lose tonight and someone stood to gain. Who needed messy emotions clouding the issue?

Larinda made herself smile at Garner. Win or lose, she wouldn't sleep with the enemy again. She'd love him, true, but only until she could force a stop to it. Garner Maycomb was a step in the right direction. He looked manageable, he was the right age and he was blond. If he liked movies, he'd be all the right stuff.

She took a seat between him and Eva to hear the committee out. The chairman, a prosperous auto dealer, made the committee's recommendation short and sweet. After summarizing every point of view expressed at the prior meeting and describing the committee's investigation and decision process, he announced its findings.

"We," he said, "unanimously recommend that permission for Ms. Outlaw's operation of the Moonglow as a drive-in movie theater be denied. A housing development's contribution to Weston's tax base cannot and should not be ignored by the council. We—"

The rest of his remarks were drowned out by cheers and applause from one half of the hall. Gasps of displeasure and disappointment sounded from the other. Within minutes the council undertook a vote and sided five-to-one against the Moonglow. Larinda shot a glare at Cash and saw him meet Cleve Davis's triumphant high five.

She turned to Eva, who looked ready to cry. "Don't give them the satisfaction," Larinda commanded, rising from her seat as the meeting came to an abrupt end. "Let's get out of here."

"Let's," Garner agreed, taking her arm and Eva's. "May I buy you both a cup of coffee—or something stronger—to drown your sorrows?"

"Not for me," said Eva, her voice shaking. "I'm going home to stick pins in my Cleve Davis voodoo doll. His greed is infecting everything from the committee to the council. Money! All this town thinks of these days is making the fastest buck." She marched off with a lace hankie pressed to her nose and Mrs. Soames clucking at her side.

"That leaves just us," Garner said after Larinda had thanked the remnant of her disappointed supporters. "May I buy *you* coffee in the shop around the corner, pretty lady?"

"After *I* introduce myself, you may," a gritty voice behind Larinda interposed. "Cleve Davis here, Miss Outlaw."

Larinda turned and saw his gloating expression as he extended a thick-fingered hand to her. "How do you do, Mr. Davis." Finding it difficult to be a good loser in light of the look on his face, she let her fingers touch his only briefly before she murmured, "Luck has been with you tonight."

"You can say that again. I hear you'll be wanting a buyer this time next year. Let's talk now. Line our ducks up, if you know what I mean."

"I'm afraid Jethro Everly's will forbids any negotiation of a sale on my part, Mr. Davis, until Mr. Bowman's lease expires."

"Hey, hey," he said, spreading his hammy hands. "Who's to know if we chat in advance?"

"I'll know."

He tapped his temple. "Think about it. Give me a call tonight, tomorrow, anytime."

"This time next year, I'll think about it." She turned to Garner, who hovered at her side, and said, "Yes, you may buy me a cup of coffee. Good night, Mr. Davis."

Davis tipped an imaginary hat and affected a courtly bow as exaggerated as it was insincere. Walking away with Garner, Larinda shivered. She wished she could wash the hand she'd extended to Davis. As Eva had asserted, greed oozed from his every pore. Larinda loathed the feel of it on her palm.

Although she felt like weeping over the outcome of the meeting, she didn't shed a tear in the course of two cups of coffee with Garner. Not once did she let on how total her disappointment was. Nor did she indicate to

Garner what a bland, blond bore she found him to be by the time he escorted her to her car. He not only loved every schmaltzy movie she had ever loathed, but loathed every quirky movie she had ever loved.

She was still holding her tears back when she returned to the Moonglow. Dan's baby-sitter's car was still outside Cash's trailer. She guessed that Cash had gone celebrating with Davis and his admirers.

Too charged with emotion to sit still, she took a quick walk around the grounds. Walt picked her out from a distance with his flashlight and waved it in an arc of greeting. She waved back.

"I heard the bad news," he said when he met up with her a minute later. "Fran called a bit ago. She's stayed out of the whole thing because of my job here, but we're both awfully sorry it didn't go your way."

Larinda tried to shrug. "The council has spoken." She looked up at the screen. "I'm sorry, too. Sorrier than I thought I'd be."

"How's that?"

"I don't know—" she looked around at the dark, uneven line of the fence "—it's begun to feel like home somehow." She thought of her sprouting garden and her flowered bedroom walls. "Leaving won't be as easy as I thought, I guess. Selling won't, either, with Cleve Davis on the buying end."

"He'll pay top dollar when the time comes, I hear."

Top dollar. Not long ago, she'd have been elated at the prospect. Now it didn't sound as terrific as it once had. Selling didn't sound as great, either. Now that she had battled side by side with many of the good people of Weston for the Moonglow, doing what she had fought for seemed like the only thing still worthwhile.

She gazed up at the screen again and saw not a ruin to be bulldozed down but the vanishing species of big-screen American movie entertainment. "There's nothing more American," Eva had said, "than cars and movies."

Larinda sighed. "Be it Davis or anyone else, I'll have to sell to *somebody* to buy the video store I want."

"Sounds like you don't want it near as much as you did at first, or do I hear wrong?"

"Who knows?" She shrugged again. "Maybe I do and don't know it."

Walt aimed his flashlight at the screen and made the beam hop from hole to hole. "Chester used to say that happiness isn't having what you want, it's—"

"Wanting what you have," Larinda dejectedly rejoined.

Walt nodded. "Not a bad way to go about living, he always said. He also said it took him most of his life to figure that out. Me, I've always thought along those lines. Enough's enough the way I see it."

"Unfortunately, what I have isn't enough, Walt."

"Enough for what?"

"Why, for . . . for . . ." She floundered, unable to reply and bewildered at why that should be.

"You and Cash," he said, shaking his head, "Neither of you know quite what you want now, do you?"

"Of course we do," she replied, recovering from her lapse. "Ours just happen to be entirely opposite wants."

"Chester'd say they wouldn't be if you both wanted what you have." Walt began moving away. "I'll mosey on. Watch out for Cash driving in. He might not be steering real straight after the celebration tonight."

Larinda watched his light bob toward the concession building. *Enough for what?* It had been a simple enough inquiry, one she'd had a ready answer for until tonight. A few hours ago there had been no question in her mind about what she wanted and why. Now there seemed to be only questions.

Planning for the renewal of the Moonglow had been a challenge, both exciting and thrilling. She missed that now, wanted it back as she had once wanted to have her video store back.

She walked on, mulling over Chester's philosophy and Walt's agreement with it. The more she thought about it, the more she realized that she'd been wanting what she had—the Moonglow—and been happy in the anticipation of its success. Except for her difficulties with Cash, her days since her return to Weston had been active and productive and, well, fun.

Could it be that she was actually feeling more disappointed over the council vote than she'd felt when she'd returned to Anaheim without Cash's lease bought out? She swallowed back a clump of tears in her throat. The lease issue had been a crusher, but this felt worse.

The Moonglow had stolen its way into her heart and displaced Outlaw Video. Just as love for Cash had stolen into her heart. She blinked against the tears that threatened.

The Moonglow and Cash Bowman, two lost causes if ever two existed.

"To the Moonglow Drive-in," Cleve Davis toasted, clinking his shot glass of rye against Cash's bottle of beer, "the best lost cause in Weston."

Knowing Cleve was too lit to notice, Cash didn't bother to drink to that as every other Davis supporter in the crowded Westonia Bar did. This was the eighth time that Cleve had proposed the same toast word for word. By the third repeat the phrase had worn thin with Cash.

He was still on his first beer, whereas Cleve had downed four shots of rye. After seeing Larinda walk out of the meeting with Garner Maycomb, Cash had walked into the Westonia intending to get rip-roaring drunk. The only thing that had stopped him was the idea of setting a bad example for Dan.

Before tonight, Cash had liked what he knew of Garner Maycomb just fine. Now the mere thought of Eva's son made him see red. *Red. What's she doing with that twirp? Where are they? If he touches one square inch of her, now or ever, I'll—*

"Know what I'm gonna do tomorrow?" Cleve asked, nudging Cash in the ribs.

"No. What?"

"Make her the best offer she's ever had."

Cash stiffened on his bar stool. "Who?"

"Outlaw." Davis licked the rim of his shot glass. "The offer is me. I'm gonna drive by tomorrow 'n sorta drop in, ya know? Get on a first-name basis with that hair. You ever see a red like that?" He smacked his lips. "Me and my boys have a bet riding on whether she's a natural redhead or not, if you know what I mean."

"Shut up, Cleve."

"Inquiring minds want to know, Bowman. Don't *you?* Or do you know and aren't tellin'?"

Cash slid off his stool. "I'm heading home."

"You want in on the odds for real or fake? Ten bucks."

"Thanks for the beer. See you around."

"Hey, when you spot my car next door, you'll know I'm finding out."

Only the thought of Dan hearing about it kept Cash from connecting a fist with Cleve's nose. He shouldered his way out of the bar. Outside, he jammed his clenched fists in his pants-pockets and strode directly to his Chevy.

He drove away so fast that his tires screeched. He was mad enough to chew bottle glass and spit roofing nails. Garner Maycomb and Tomcat Davis had better watch their step. If either of them touched Larinda, they'd live to regret it.

Cash calmed a little when he got home. It helped to see no car but Larinda's at her place and her lights on inside. Once the baby-sitter left, he had to pretend to be calm for Dan.

"How come you're still up, Scout?"

"Couldn't go to sleep. I only like it if Larinda takes care of me."

"You aren't her responsibility, Dan."

"How come?"

"Don't nag your worn-out old dad to death. Want a cup of cocoa?"

Dan brightened. "Have one with me?"

"Sure." Cash put water on to heat and emptied packets of instant hot chocolate into two mugs. Drinking with Dan was infinitely preferable to bending an elbow with Cleve Davis. "Go get one of your animal books and we'll look through it together."

Dan ran to his bedroom and came back with a stack of books. "I checked 'em out at school today," he said, pulling one out of the stack. "This one's the neatest, *California's Wild Heritage*."

Cash poured heated water into the mugs, stirred, and set one down in front of Dan at the table. "Sounds wild enough." He sat across from Dan with his own cocoa. "What's in it?"

"Everything." Dan flipped the big book open and thumbed to a glossy photo of a fish. "Did you know Chinook salmon swim in the Sacramento River?"

Cash shook his head. "What else don't I know?"

"Lots." Dan turned the book around for Cash to see a photo of a bird. "That's a marbled murrelet." He turned several more pages. "This is a San Joaquin kit fox. Just like the foxes in the big field outside," he added.

Cash had heard of the foxes more than once from his son. He privately discounted them now as he'd done before after several of the local farmers had assured him that foxes were long gone from the area. "Farther up in the foothills you'll see one now and then," one farmer had said, "but not down here anymore."

"There're two out there," Dan said, his eyes shining. "They have babies now. I'll show you tomorrow, okay?"

"Tomorrow's Thursday, Scout. I have market."

"I'll show you Friday after school, then. Maybe Larinda can come, too."

"Uh, let's keep it just guys, Dan. The council didn't vote the way she hoped they would tonight."

Dan looked stricken. "They won't let her put on Roadrunner cartoons? And old movies like *Dick Tracy*?"

"Not unless Davis Development decides not to build houses, and that's not going to happen. One of them will be ours if we're lucky." He mussed up Dan's hair with one hand. "Drink up. It's past your bedtime."

After Dan had trudged to bed and fallen asleep, Cash settled down to study. But his mind was too full of Larinda to concentrate. He stared at textbook pages that made no sense. What was he studying, and why? When had getting a college degree begun to seem less urgent than it had previously? When had everything he'd wanted begun to seem less important than spending a lifetime of nights like the one he'd spent with her?

He should be savoring victory, yet he felt defeated. In retrospect, siding with Cleve Davis hadn't been his finest moment. Aside from his own interest in wanting Larinda's plan blocked, Cash had always known Cleve's driving motive was greed.

He hadn't thought that Cleve's ambitions would extend to Larinda herself.

He clapped his book shut. If Cleve came drooling within ten feet of her, he'd regret it. The same went for Garner Maycomb.

LARINDA WATCHED out her kitchen window on Friday as Cash and Dan set off together across the nearest field. Cash had a pair of binoculars slung around his neck. Dan had a camera hung around his. He had told her earlier that he'd take a picture of the baby foxes for her to tape to her refrigerator. She hadn't had the heart to tell him not to bother, since she intended to have her trailer towed to Anaheim in a few days. She'd decided to live there rather than next door to Cash.

She had spent yesterday and most of today looking
for a job in Weston. She couldn't see herself doing anything that was available. The local video stores needed
low-paid clerks, but no managers. In the L.A. area she'd
be able to find a management position, but Weston was
too small.

Most of all, she couldn't see herself living next door
to Cash for a year. He had aided in her defeat to serve
his own ends. He had slept with her one night and stood
against her the next. And she'd done the same to him.
There could be nothing but cold war between her and
Cash. It was no way to live.

By the end of next week she and her trailer would be
gone. Weston's loss would be Anaheim's gain. She'd
come back next year, sell to Cleve Davis and be on her
way. In that year, she'd get over Cash.

Her phone rang. She turned away from the window
to answer it. The caller was Cleve Davis.

"Hey, hey," he said. "Where've you been the past two
days?"

"Here and there. Why?"

"I dropped by twice. No one home, just Bowman
skulking around next door looking ready to pop me
one. You and him have a thing going, by any chance?"

"No." *Not anymore.*

"That's what I figured. Say, how's about dinner tonight and we do some talking?"

"Mr. Davis, the terms of Jethro's will—"

"Will, shmill," he cut in dismissively. "Who says we
have to talk real estate? We can talk anything you like
over a couple of steaks and a few drinks. You like
steak?" He didn't pause for her answer. "I know a place

you can get one big and meaty." His tone dropped several notes. "My place. How's about it?"

"I take it your wife is cooking, Mr. Davis?"

"'Cleve' is the name, Larinda. *My* place isn't where Barbi and myself live."

"I see. Where is *your* place?"

"I'll pick you up around seven and show you. Seven okay with you?"

"No. I don't date married men, Mr. Davis. And regarding the land I'll be selling, don't call me, I'll call you—next year. Until then, goodbye."

She hung up. The phone rang again ten seconds later. She let it ring. If it was Cleve again, or Garner Maycomb for the third time since the night of the meeting, she wasn't interested.

What *did* interest her was Cleve's mention of Cash lurking around looking dangerous. Cash jealous? He hadn't said a word to her since the night in her bed. He hadn't looked once across the garden rows at her. His last look had been nothing more than the quick glance she'd caught in passing as she walked out of city hall with Garner.

Cash jealous. The idea that his primitive instincts were involved thrilled her as much as it upset her. She shouldn't feel touched by his male posturing. He was still a man she couldn't otherwise trust.

Even so, as a woman, she wasn't immune to the primal appeal of a strong male whose protective instincts had been aroused. How could she dam the flood of excitement that welled up when she thought about how Cash had been spoiling to punch Cleve off her doorstep?

She couldn't.

12

CASH TRAINED his binoculars on the grove of cotton-wood trees Dan was pointing out.

"See the burrow under the biggest tree, Dad?"

"Yeah, I think so." He didn't see a damn thing but rocks and humps of weedy grass under the trees, but if Dan believed foxes burrowed there, let him. Cash fine-tuned the focus. A big rock filled his frame of vision, then a tuft of weeds, then a—"Hey!"

"See it?"

"The burrow is the hole by the big rock?"

"That's it. See any foxes?"

"Not yet." Nor did Cash expect to see any, although a small cavelike opening was visible next to the rock under the tallest tree. He could understand that a small boy might imagine it to be a fox burrow. He caught his breath, as a black-tipped nose pushed out of the hole. Focusing better, he saw pointed ears emerge, followed by a furred body and plumed tail.

Cash lowered the field glasses and looked at Dan in awe. "Damned if it isn't a fox."

"Told ya. Let me see." Dan took the binoculars from Cash. "That's the mother. Here comes a baby." He let Cash have a look.

"Well, son of a gun," Cash said, watching a ball of fur tumble out, followed by another. "*Two* babies."

Dan had already shown him a killdeer's nest and a swampy area nearby that was home to swarms of water bugs and schools of tadpoles. They had been interesting, but not like this.

Dan nodded, too. "They're different from other kinds of foxes. You can tell by their fur and everything. You stay here," he said. "I'll get closer and take pictures. They're pretty used to me now."

Cash had to marvel at the ease with which Dan stealthfully wiggled on his belly through knee-high alfalfa. When he got close enough, he snapped several shots of the foxes. The kid was really something for a seven-year-old. Cash felt a rush of love and pride.

Grinning, Dan wiggled back with the camera, then paused with Cash for a final gaze through the binoculars. "Next," he said, leading Cash away, "I'll show you a trap-door spider. Larinda said 'Holy moley' when she saw the door open."

Larinda again. Dan had chatted about her constantly during the walk today, describing everything she had said and done each time he'd brought her out and showed her nature's secrets. It hadn't done Cash a lot of good to hear so much about her. But he wanted to hear more.

"What did she say when she saw the foxes, Dan?"

"I forgot the binoculars, so she couldn't see. I'll bring her tomorrow, maybe."

Cash slowed his pace. "You know, Scout, it might be a good thing if you stopped seeing so much of her. She . . . well, she might not be here much longer."

"Why not?" Dan stopped, his lower lip quivering.

"Because living here isn't going to suit her if she can't show movies," Cash said gently, kneeling to face Dan,

"You'll need to get used to her being gone. I may be wrong about her leaving, of course, but—"

"Where's she gonna go?"

"Most likely back to Anaheim, since that's where her family lives. She'll probably take her trailer there."

Tears wobbled in Dan's eyes. "I don't want her to go. Do you?"

Cash pulled in a deep, thick breath as he gathered Dan into his arms for a hard, wet cry. "Not as much as I once did," he admitted. "I'll miss her, too."

He knew he was in trouble when he heard his voice break on the last word. He knew he was in love. It'd feel like the end of the world when Larinda Outlaw hitched up her trailer and left him and Dan and the Moonglow behind.

"Make her stay," Dan blubbered into Cash's shoulder. "Mom never stayed with us, but Larinda would if you made her."

"Dan, I can't. Your mother had to do what she had to do. So does Larinda."

"If you got married to her, she wouldn't go."

Cash felt his eyes go moist. "I'm the last man on earth she'd marry." He pulled a handkerchief out of his back pocket. "Here. Blow your nose and try not to feel too bad."

Dan blew into the handkerchief. "How come you're the last man?"

"Because grown-ups get mad at each other just like kids do. They say things they shouldn't say and do things they shouldn't do. Before they know it, they—"

"Grown-ups make kids 'pologize," Dan cut in solemnly. "I had to say 'I'm sorry' at school *three* times."

"Look, why don't we go back home and read all about the foxes we just saw, okay?"

Dan heaved a long, sad sigh. "Okay. My book says they mate for life. Not like people, huh?"

"Lots of people mate for life." Cash took Dan's hand and started walking back the way they'd come. "Your mother wasn't one of them," he added, "but millions around the world do."

Cash thought about mating for life with Larinda. It shouldn't have seemed like the best thing he'd ever thought, yet it did. It was also the most damn-fool, hopeless, impossible thing a man in his situation should be thinking.

THE THOUGHT was still plaguing his mind when he and Dan sat down to read about foxes in *California's Wild Heritage* after their walk home.

"Here's the same kind of fox, right on the book cover," Dan said. "See?"

Too full of thoughts of Larinda to more than half see, Cash murmured, "That's it, all right." Marriage was the riskiest proposition on earth, he was thinking. After failing at one, it was the last thing he should be considering.

Dan pointed to the subtitle under the main title on the glossy book jacket. "What's this big word?"

Cash had to shift out of his train of thought at that inquiry. "That big word is—" His eyes widened at what that big word, and the one following it, was. "It's—" No, it couldn't be. "Let's look at the Chinook salmon again," he said to divert Dan's attention elsewhere as quickly as he could.

Dan eagerly opened the book, then looked up and frowned at Cash. "You feel sick, Dad?"

"Uhhhhh . . ." Cash felt hot and cold by turns at the subtitle he had just read. "Errrr . . ."

"You look sick."

"No, no, I'm not. I'm just . . ."

"You look all weirded out."

Cash bit his lower lip and got his expression back in order. "I feel fine." He waited until Dan was engrossed in the salmon before he asked as casually as possible, "Um, Dan, how long have you had this book?"

"Couple of days."

"Have you shown it to Larinda?"

"Nope. Not yet."

"Well, how about if you don't show it to her." Cash nervously rubbed his chin. "Okay?"

"How come?"

"So we can keep it a guy's thing. Like our walk today, and seeing the foxes, and the guy-to-guy talks we've had and stuff like that. You know."

"Like the egg and the sperms, you mean?" Dan inquired with a wink of male conspiracy.

"Exactly like that. Just between us."

"Okay. My teacher said to bring the book back Monday, anyway."

"Good." Cash breathed an inner sigh of relief. If Larinda got a close look at the book, and if its subtitle meant what it said, she might put two and two together. If she did, Weston and the town council would be in an uproar again.

CASH FOUND IT increasingly difficult to live with the discovery he had made. He found it just as difficult to live with the idea of Larinda going away. On Saturday morning she walked into his office and announced her intention to move back to Anaheim.

"I'll be leaving a week from now," she said without any preliminary pleasantries, "and taking my trailer with me. It's more than my car can pull, so I've lined up a trucker to tow it down. As for my garden, I'll keep it going if you want to take it over after I'm gone."

"I wouldn't mind," he said with a shrug to hide the effect of the blow she'd dealt him. He'd been expecting it, sure, but that didn't soften the impact when he actually heard the words.

"Well, then, that's all I came to say, except that I'm driving home tomorrow for two days to rent a trailer space and see my brother before he's off for boot camp." She rose from the chair she'd barely perched on. "Shall I tell Dan what's going to happen or would you rather do it?"

"I already mentioned that you might move, so he's halfway prepared."

"How did he react?"

"Tears. He likes you a lot."

"I like him a lot, too. Where is he, by the way?"

"He's busy polishing Bartley's apples. I'm not looking forward to telling him you'll be gone for sure. He'll . . . he'll miss you."

"I'll tell him myself when the time is right. I'll miss him, too, very much."

"Like you won't miss me?" Cash asked, looking down at his hands on the desk.

"I didn't say I wouldn't. You did." Larinda turned to go, then half turned back. "You won't miss me either, I expect."

Cash looked up. "I didn't say that. You did."

"In any event, there's not much else to say, is there?"

"Maybe there's a lot," he retorted with a glance at his open door, "but now's not the time for it."

Larinda lifted her chin and moved to the door. "A little or a lot, I doubt that we'd end up agreeing with each other if we ever said any of it."

"That *is* the way it's always gone with us," Cash muttered in bitter agreement.

"Have a good week," she threw back as she walked out.

"You, too." He knew he'd have a rotten week, every day and every night. And knowing what he now knew would make them twice as difficult as before.

THAT EVENING after he closed the market, fed Dan dinner and put him to sleep, Cash sat down with Dan's book. Handling it like a stick of dynamite, he opened it and started reading. The more he read of one particular section, the more he wanted to turn a blind eye to every word and heart-tugging photo it contained.

After he'd read enough to wish he'd never opened the book, he went out to polish the Chevy and wrestle with his conscience. It was hell knowing he could say a few words at the next council meeting and possibly change the entire complexion of Cleve Davis's development plans. Larinda's plan could find itself back in the realm of possibility the moment he opened his mouth.

He tried to think straight about what that would mean. She'd stay and show movies. He'd endure the hassle and take the necessary cut in profits. In a year, she'd sell out. A lot could happen in a year. She could begin wanting to show movies forever, just as he'd begun wanting to run the flea market for a lot longer than he'd originally thought.

He wasn't sure he was still thinking straight, when it struck him that the Moonglow would make a nice living for a family of three.

Damn. Why were there no easy answers when it came to women? He loved the one next door, there was no getting around it. It had been growing in him as surely as her garden was growing greener every day. But did she love him? If she did, he'd be smart to speak up at the next council meeting. If she didn't, he'd be smart to forget every word and photo in that damned book.

Fine time for love to be making him think Chester's philosophy had the ring of truth to it. Running the flea market on a long-term basis would be wanting what he had. For Larinda, running the drive-in would be wanting what *she* had.

He polished and thought and decided that he couldn't make the next move without knowing whether she loved him or not. To find out as soon as he needed to know, he'd have to ask. One week and she'd be gone. He'd have to ask before then if he wanted badly enough to know.

He glanced at her trailer. Her lights were on. She was up, maybe watching TV, maybe reading, maybe counting the days until she'd be leaving. Leaving . . .

How could he walk in and ask point-blank if she loved him? He couldn't. Women in love didn't say "Have a nice week" and mean "I love you" by it. Did they? He wiped his dampening palms on the chamois polishing cloth.

Asking would be like cutting down a giant fir without knowing where it would fall. For courage, a man would need a brandy first. He went inside and poured a hefty one. He was halfway through it when a knock sounded on his door.

"Can we talk?" Larinda said when he opened it. "Out here, if Dan's asleep."

Noting the half-empty wineglass in her hand and the reckless look on her face, Cash tightened his fingers on his brandy glass. "Are you drunk?"

"On half a glass? No." She looked at the drink in his hand. "Are you?"

"No." He stepped out and closed the door behind him. "Talk about what?"

"Us."

"Where do you want to start?" he asked, sitting down on his front step.

Larinda sat down half-facing him. "Let's start with the night we made love."

"Which one?"

"The last one. You slept all night with me, but what did I find in the morning? Nothing. Never mind what happened after that with the council voting me down. I'd just like to know why I woke up alone."

"I had school and I . . . didn't know what to say."

"Anything would have been better than nothing. I felt used. Was I?"

"Used? How do you think *I* felt when you took off with Garner the other night?" he shot back. "'Used' is putting it mildly, Red."

"Are you saying you're jealous, Cash?"

He shook his head. "Only a man with love on his agenda can be jealous. I can't afford to be in love with a woman who's putting me out of work in a year."

Larinda sat in subdued silence after he said that. She stared for several moments into her wine. Very deliberately she then set it aside. "Could you spare me a sip of your brandy?"

Cash handed it to her and watched her lips as she took one, two, three sips. He saw her dark lashes sweep up as she gave him a direct look of longing over the rim of his glass. Her expression made him curl his hand around hers where she held his brandy.

"Hell, yes, I was jealous," he admitted in a harsh, hissing whisper. He sank his gaze into hers. "I'm jealous right now just thinking about him." He felt her hand shake under his.

"He means nothing to me," she whispered.

"What do *I* mean to you, Red?"

"More than you should. Love isn't on my agenda any more than it's on yours."

Larinda didn't know where the glass tumbled to when Cash jerked her into his arms. Its fate was her last concern, the first being the heaven of his mouth on hers. She was starved for him, as needy in her response as he was in consuming his share of the long, deep kiss.

He ended it with a liquid moan and held her slightly away. "That's what you mean to me, Red. What else did you want to discuss?"

"I'm not sure now." She pulled back farther to catch her breath.

"Let's talk more about *us*," he suggested. "There's something strong between us. It's enough to make me think my father was right about wanting what you have. Lately, I've been thinking . . ."

"What?"

He shook his head and released her. "What I've been thinking isn't what you want."

"What makes you feel Chester was right?"

Hell, Cash thought. *Do I have anything to lose that I won't lose if she moves to Anaheim?* "Red, what if I decided I'd rather work the flea market more than anything else—assuming the place didn't get sold out from under me." He was careful not to look her way when he warily added, "What if you didn't sell the Moonglow next year? What if you were able to show movies and decided to do that on a permanent basis?"

Larinda couldn't help edging away, her response cool. "The stand you took with Cleve Davis certainly removed the chance of any of those 'what ifs' coming to pass. Even if I wanted to keep the Moonglow now and operate it the way I planned to, I can't."

"Would you want to if you could, Red?"

"Maybe," she hedged. "I've been thinking, too, that wanting what I have wouldn't be a minus if . . ." She hesitated, debating how much she should say of what had been on her mind lately.

"If what?"

"Well, if you ran the flea market and I ran the drive-in and we could work it all out without strangling each other over it. But there's no chance of it now that everything's said and done."

Cash gave her a guarded, sidelong glance. "What if there was a chance?"

"There might have been one at the beginning," she granted. "Things might have evolved in that direction if we'd both wanted what we had then, but we didn't."

"We wanted one thing we had then, Red. We wanted each other."

"Not enough to agree on anything but that," Larinda countered. "It wasn't enough for you to resist going behind my back with Davis. If you hadn't done that, running the drive-in and flea market long-term might have been possible"

"Red, Davis would have opposed you and won with or without me."

"Even before that," she retorted, "you weren't a man I could trust. In any event, whatever might have been is history, now."

"Funny," he murmured, "you just kissed me as if you loved me."

"Maybe I do, but I don't trust you. Not after all that's happened."

Cash gripped her by the shoulders and turned her to face him on the step. "You gave me as much reason to stand against you as I gave you to mistrust me. But I want to put things right between us now—if you want it, too."

"How?"

"Never mind how. Just promise me you aren't one for the money like you were before. Say you'll keep the Moonglow on a permanent basis if I give you proof positive that you can trust me."

"Cash, start making sense. I can't keep the Moonglow unless I operate it and the council isn't going to change its mind."

"What if I changed it for them?"

"How?"

"I love you, Red." He planted a hard, hot kiss on her lips. "Do you love me?"

"I . . . answer me first. How?"

"Do you or don't you love me?"

"What if I do?"

"Yes or no?"

She looked deep into his eyes and weakened. "Yes, but how do you expect to—?"

"If you love me, say you'll keep the Moonglow. Say it and I'll give you every reason on earth to trust me no matter what happens. Just—" he breathed deep "—say it."

His grip was too compelling, his gaze too intense to resist. "Very well, I'll keep it, if possible. What do you mean 'no matter what happens'?"

"Say you'll renew my lease, too."

"Cash, you don't make a bit of sense."

"Neither does this," he said, kissing her again until she emerged dizzy from it. "Say you'll renew my lease if I give you reason to trust me."

Pushing him away so she could see, if not think straight, she waveringly agreed, "I'll renew it if you do, but I still don't see how you intend to—"

"You'll see," Cash cut in, "at the special council meeting."

"What special council meeting?"

"The one I'm going to call for Monday night." He stood, drawing her up with him. "Be there."

"How can I? I'm driving home tomorrow to locate a space for my trailer and see my brother, who's leaving this weekend to join the army. Remember?"

Cash frowned at that unwelcome reminder. "When will you be back?"

"On Tuesday."

"Be there Tuesday night, then. How early are you leaving tomorrow?"

"Very. I want to be with Larson a few days before he goes. He's the only brother I have."

"Too early to spend some time in the back seat now with me, Red?"

"Cash, everything still stands between us, even though we've talked. Making love would just make it worse when I hitch up next week and go."

"A flimsy excuse if I ever heard one," he protested, pulling her close. "Haven't you been crawling the walls every night like me? Haven't you been wanting your next-door neighbor closer than this? Haven't you?"

"Maybe I have, but there's still Dan to consider," she cautioned. "If he chanced to look out his window and saw us, I'd never forgive us."

"You're talking like a good mother."

"You're not talking like a good father."

"What about when you come back, Red?" He slid his hands down her spine and cupped her hips forward until the notch of her thighs was right where he was rigid with desire. "What if Dan stays at Jeffie's Tuesday night so we can be alone?"

She squirmed in his hands. "Cash, what sense is there in making love now or then with no hope of things lasting?"

"He'll stay at Jeffie's Tuesday night," Cash resolved. "After the meeting, we'll make love. Just be there...and trust me."

13

EMOTIONALLY CONFUSED and sexually frustrated, Larinda drove to Anaheim the next morning. She couldn't begin to believe that anything would happen to change the council's vote. Nor could she believe that Cash had said he loved her. Thinking back on her own hesitant admission of love and the promises she'd made at his insistence, she wasn't sure of herself or of what to believe anymore.

How could she be in love? How could Cash? What lapse in judgment had lured such fateful words from their lips? Thankfully, it hadn't extended to making love there on his front step. It had come close enough, however, that she blushed all the way to Anaheim at what Walt would have seen if he'd passed by.

Cash had as few inhibitions when it came to saying goodnight on a doorstep as he'd had in bed. It had taken her a long, breathless while to finally part from kisses too delicious to leave untasted.

His hot whispers about what he'd do with her when she got back had thrilled her into lingering that much longer to hear more. He had nibbled the curve of her ear and whispered that he intended to find a secluded spot where he'd spread her out on the hood of his Chevy under the light of the moon.

"Think about it. Red on red," he had murmured, then went on to describe how he'd touch and where he'd kiss and what she'd feel when he did it all.

She hoped her parents and brother wouldn't see the look of love in her eyes. She didn't yet trust that she truly loved Cash, or that he loved her, either. Explaining any of it to her family would be as impossible as explaining it to herself. She was having trouble enough figuring out how to tell them that she wouldn't be showing *Wild West*—or any other movie—at the Moonglow.

Larry and Linda came out the door the minute she drove up to the curb. Larson was close behind them.

"Soon to be a soldier boy, huh?" Larinda said to him after hugs of greeting and welcome from each of them.

"Day after tomorrow," Larson replied. "What happened to the grand opening you weren't going to have without me?"

"I'll explain at lunch."

He peered into her face. "What agrees with you in Weston? The weather or a guy?"

"A guy, we hope," Larry said, then glanced at his wife. "Grandchildren are looking scarcer than ever around here."

"I'm not the only potential parent in this crowd," Larinda retorted with a nudge to her brother's ribs.

"Well, I hope both potential parents are hungry," said her mother, "I'm making pot roast and gravy for lunch."

Larson rubbed his stomach. "When I think about boot camp, pot roast gives me reason to celebrate." He ceremoniously offered his mother his arm on the way back into the house. "Can we eat early and all day long?"

Larinda followed them with her father.

"*Is* it a man who's got your eyes smiling again, Rinda?" her father murmured, lagging behind for a moment. "You have the look of a flower garden in bloom."

She hedged, "Isn't that appropriate in the springtime?"

"The rose in your cheek and the sparkle in your eye got there all by themselves, girl?"

"It's your overactive imagination. Look to Larson for grandchildren, not me."

"He's still a child, himself. Is Cash Bowman the lucky man responsible for your glow, Rinda?"

"It's that time of year, Daddy, nothing more."

The dubious rise of his eyebrows said he didn't believe a word she'd spoken. "You looked almost this pink the last time you drove down from Weston. It seemed too soon to comment then, but not now. What's wrong that you don't want us to know the good news?"

"Everything." She threw up her hands in defeat. "Cash is already a father, not blond, doesn't know movies and can't be trusted by anyone like me so far."

"Doesn't know *movies?*" Larry looked mildly shocked. "Not even *Wild West?*"

"Not even the Outlaw family's only claim to fame," Larinda confirmed, holding the front door open for her father to follow her in. "Can we drop the subject now that it's exhausted?"

"What subject?" Linda inquired over her shoulder on her way into the kitchen.

"The man in her life," Larry replied.

"Man?" Linda stopped and turned with a big smile on her face." Did you say 'man'?"

Larinda rolled her eyes. "Larson, will you restrain our mother from drooling all over her apron?"

"Did you say 'man'?" Larson echoed with exaggerated interest.

Larinda very deliberately stepped on her brother's foot as she pushed past him and her mother into the kitchen. "What's for dessert?" she inquired sweetly. "Pie, I hope. Hurray, it is. What kind?"

Right on her heels in bright-eyed anticipation, her mother replied, "Banana cream. Who don't you want to tell us about, Rinda?"

"He's not blond, she says," Larry volunteered. "I say what does that matter if he can put a sparkle like that in a woman's eye?"

Her mother nodded. "That's a sparkle I see, all right. Who put it there, Rinda? Cash Bowman, I'll bet. How is his son, Dan?"

"Mom and Dad are closing in for the kill," Larson advised with a wink.

Larinda replied, "It's all an act with them. You can take actors out of acting, but you can't take acting out of actors. They can do entire ham-it-up scenes like this in their sleep."

"Only because we've had years of rehearsal since you came of grandchild-bearing age," Linda sniffed as she bustled around the kitchen checking the roast and stirring the gravy. "Everyone we know has grandchildren, don't they, Larry?"

He nodded. "Just about. The rest spend their time wishing like we do."

Larinda threw up her hands, defeated again. "Cash Bowman put me out of business a few days ago. Because of a greedy land developer and him, I won't be reopening the Moonglow. Nothing I planned before I left here will happen now. He's as untrustworthy as the day is long and last night he tried to convince me I should trust him. After everything he's done to thwart me, I should trust him?"

"I'd say she's in love," Larry said to Linda.

"I'd say she is, too." Linda arched a glance at Larson. "What's your vote while we're counting?"

Larson nodded in agreement. "The L word, no doubt about it. Why didn't you drag Bowman home with you and introduce him around, Sis? We'd be cool."

"This is the last place I'd bring a marriageable male, with you three breathing down my neck."

Larinda had to break down and laugh then, at them and herself for thinking she could withstand them. As financially precarious as life in the Outlaw household had often been, it had never been boring or short on humor. Her parents' flair for drama and comedy had seen to that, if not to keeping the family finances on an even keel.

Over lunch, she ended up telling them and Larson a bit about her stormy relationship with Cash. She talked about Dan, too, and Walt, Fran and Eva. She concluded with the council vote and its nearly unanimous decision in favor of Cleve Davis. Her family shook their heads in disappointment.

Frowning, her father inquired, "Cash stood against you with the land man?"

"Shoulder to shoulder," Larinda affirmed. "See why I don't—and can't—trust him an inch?"

"Yes, but are you in love with him?" her mother most pointedly wanted to know.

Larinda rolled her eyes. "What does that matter?"

"It's the most important thing, Rinda," her father replied. "Your mother and I don't always agree, but we've always been in love. How else would we iron the wrinkles out? If you and Cash are in love—"

"Cash and I have far too many wrinkles to be in love."

Linda fixed her with a knowing gaze. "You don't look all that certain of it. Could you come back here and forget him deep in your heart?"

"Maybe not entirely," Larinda had to admit. They were wearing her down, making her acknowledge her true feelings to them—and to herself. "Maybe I don't honestly know."

"Somewhere deep inside you do, Rinda," Larry said.

Linda nodded. "Somewhere you know if it's true love."

"Guess where," her brother put in with a salacious shimmy of his eyebrows and a wicked grin. "One guess."

Larinda couldn't resist playing mean big sister to his bratty little brother. "Go back to licking your plate clean, pip-squeak."

"Mother, may I?" Larson requested of his mother in a squeaky falsetto.

"Clean your plates? Of course you may, both of you," Linda said, rising from her chair. "Come, my darling," she said to her husband. "Why waste our hard-earned wisdom on the young when we can nap while they wash the dishes?"

Larry rose, a sexy gleam in his eye. "Why, indeed? Let us 'nap.'"

Larinda and Larson watched as Larry and Linda waltzed romantically through the door and down the hall to their bedroom.

Larson exaggerated a dramatic sigh. "When we're their age, is sex, sex, sex all we'll think of, too?"

"It's all *I* think of." Larinda tried to make it sound like a wisecrack as she piled plates and saucers in tidy stacks.

"Me, too, but what guy my age doesn't?" Larson began collecting silverware. "If you're doing more than thinking in Weston maybe it *is* true love for you this time."

"Have you ever been truly in love, little brother?"

"Sure. Lots of times, big sister."

"I'm talking love, you teenage sex animal."

"A sex animal willing to sacrifice his life for his country if he has to," he reminded her in his own defense.

"Seriously, Larson."

"Oh. Well, you're a better topic for discussion than me in the love department. I've never seen you so . . ."

"'Confused' is the word."

He nodded. "Is the sex great? Seriously."

"Why do you ask at your tender young age?"

"Because I'm old enough to know great from not so great. Dad once told me, man to man, that great sex was a big factor in marriage. Look at him and Mom. It must have helped them get over the rough spots."

Larinda had a ready response. "What saved them was welfare and food stamps until they got unstarstruck and worked their way into the deli business. You came along too late to remember the worst years, little brother. Anyway, are you really old enough to know great sex from otherwise, Larson?"

He gave her a cheeky grin and pretended to buff his nails on the front of his shirt. "I've never wasted much of the time I've spent at the drive-in movies, Sis."

"You sound a lot like Cash in that department."

"Would I like him and his kid?"

She had to admit that he would. "Too much for me to drag them home and introduce them around unless I meant something by it," she told him. "But right now I feel that moving back here is the smartest thing I could do for myself."

"My room's free beginning the day after tomorrow if you want it."

"I have four of my own rooms in my trailer, thank you." She thought of the bathroom where she had showered with Cash and the bedroom where she had made love with him. Tow those rooms with the memories they contained to a trailer park in Anaheim, where there was no Cash next door? Could she last without him as long as a week, much less a year?

It shouldn't hurt so much to be apart from him at the present moment. She'd done it before and managed. But how?

"Is he nuts about you, Sis?"

"He assured me last night that he is."

"If you're nuts about him, what else do you need?"

"More than great sex and last-minute promises." She handed him soapy plates to rinse and dry. "More than he's given me so far."

"What did he promise you?"

"The impossible. The more I think about it, the more I know I wasn't thinking right last night when he sounded convincing enough to believe."

She took up a clean towel to help Larson dry. "That's enough about me. Let's talk about you. Where will you be stationed after boot camp?"

"Only army brass knows, Sis."

"Not a combat zone, I hope." She gazed at her brother with deep concern in her eyes. "Anywhere but a combat zone, okay?"

"You promised you wouldn't worry, Rinda."

"So?" she said, flinging her arms around him for a tight hug. "I'm breaking my promise, soldier boy. If you get yourself hurt or worse, I'll never forgive you."

BY THE NEXT DAY, Larson's second last as a civilian for two years, Larinda had convinced herself that Cash had been talking nonsense. But she didn't have time to dwell on it. Larson had elected to spend several of his final hours of nonmilitary freedom with her, Larry and Linda at Disneyland.

She didn't have time to dwell on it the day after that, either. Before Larson left, she rented a space in a nearby mobile home park for her trailer. In the afternoon her parents closed the deli early, and Larinda went with them and Larson to the airport where he would fly away to basic training camp. Three hours after his scheduled departure, she was still waiting with them for the delayed flight to arrive.

As she waited, she remembered Cash saying, "Just be there . . . and trust me."

She shook her head. After all that had happened, what could happen now to really change anything? It was easy, she thought, for her parents to say nothing mattered but love. Larry and Linda had always been romantics. All actors were, as far as Larinda was concerned. Stage and film weren't the real world.

The real world was a hurricane laying waste to everything in its path. It was a man and a woman battling each other for financial survival. It was the town council voting for Weston's suburbanization instead of the Moonglow's preservation. Happy endings in the real world were few and far between.

Larinda checked her watch. Soon it would be too late for any hope of driving to Weston in time for the town council meeting. She thought of the many 'what ifs' Cash had posed between kisses when she'd last seen him. She thought of the kisses. She thought about never being kissed like that again.

"It's about time," Larson said, rising from his seat next to her.

Realizing that his flight had just been announced, she stood, too. Her throat tightened. Her baby brother belonged to his country now.

"'Bye, Sis," he said, enveloping her in a big hug.

Her tearful mother got the next hug, her choked-up father the last. Larinda stood with them then and watched Larson approach the boarding gate. A cocky smile, a wave of his hand, and he was gone.

Larinda had a sudden thought of Cash being gone like that. She thought of never seeing him again. Of never seeing Dan again.

She told herself she'd simply seen too many old war movies.

The drive home from the airport with Larry and Linda was marked by long, somber silences. Larinda felt badly that she'd be departing, too, as soon as she got back to Anaheim.

"Maybe I should stay tonight," she said from the back seat.

Linda glanced back. "What about that special town meeting you mentioned the other day at lunch? You said you promised you'd be there."

"Don't stay on our account," Larry said. "Tonight we'll do what we always do when we feel bad—go to a movie."

Linda nodded. "A happy one."

Larinda checked her watch again. "If I drive without stopping, the meeting will be half over before I get there."

"What's it about, Rinda?"

"I don't know. Cash just said I'd trust him after the meeting was over."

"Maybe you should put some trust in him now, *before* it's over, Rinda."

"I've never met a man I could trust—except you and Larson, Daddy."

There was silence in the front seat for a long moment. Then her mother said softly, "If you love Cash Bowman, you already trust him somewhere in your heart."

14

LARINDA DIDN'T STOP anywhere on the route to Weston. Just getting there on time had been her aim when she'd first started out. Staying there for good became her goal by mid-trip.

Alone on the road, with four hours to think, she reviewed Larry and Linda's advice. She reflected on the past few months of her life and her feelings for Cash. Her days in Anaheim had proven to her how deep those emotions ran. She had spent much of her time missing Cash or Dan.

She'd wished for Cash's arms around her at the airport to comfort the emotional wrench she'd felt at seeing Larson leave for military duty.

"Don't mind us and our nagging about grandkids," her mother had said before she'd left. "We're happy if you're happy."

"What if happiness means wanting what I have in Weston?" she had hesitantly inquired.

"Meaning Cash and Daniel Bowman, Rinda?"

"Maybe. What would you think?"

"Be still our hearts," Linda and Larry had replied in unison, clutching at their chests.

As she neared Weston, her heart warmed at the thought of Cash and Dan meeting her family. The thought of the three of them becoming a family someday filled her with joy.

She loved Cash. How simple and self-evident it suddenly seemed. It wasn't a decision, for she hadn't arrived at it by any discernible means. No logic she could identify had led her to it. It just *was*.

Did she trust him, though? In many ways she did, now that she thought about it. She trusted him to be a good father, to be a good businessman and to be financially astute, as he'd been from the first moment she'd met him. She'd even begun to trust his capacity for fidelity, she realized. He had no reputation for fooling around; he hadn't even kissed Connie Maycomb goodnight.

Greater trust could be built on that foundation, couldn't it? In many ways, she hadn't been seeing the forest for the trees. She loved him. He wasn't perfect, but in so many ways he was worthy of trust.

As soon as she could, she told herself, she'd call the manager of the mobile-home park and say she'd decided against renting space there.

Larinda now wished she were flying, instead of driving, to tell Cash she wanted to stay and work things out with him. How little the council's decision mattered now that she knew her heart and where it belonged. Selling the Moonglow in a year didn't matter anymore, either. The flea market was Cash's livelihood. How could she sell it out from under him without a thought for his and Dan's future?

She couldn't. And wouldn't. She'd keep it and work in Weston at odd jobs if necessary until she and Cash were back on their feet and planning their future together. Only then would she consider putting her inheritance up for sale. Together with Cash she would make that decision.

Together. She guided her car off the freeway onto the Weston exit. The clock on her dashboard said she'd be late for the council meeting. She wished she had thought to call Cash before leaving, but she hadn't. She had to trust him to be there as he'd said he'd be.

"WHERE IS SHE, Dad?" Dan squirmed in his seat next to Cash.

"I wish I knew, Scout."

All around, Cash could feel the eyes of his fellow townspeople on him as they waited for the council meeting to start. Cleve and Barbi Davis were there, seated directly behind him. Eva Maycomb sat nearby. Mrs. Soames, Lonnie Lonsdale and the Purvis brothers were there, too. As far as Cash could tell, everyone from the last meeting was back in full force tonight.

He felt the silent questions each Westonian in the crowded hall was directing at him. Why had he gathered them here? Why were they and the council waiting at his nervous request for Larinda Outlaw to arrive before he'd explain?

Behind him, Cleve Davis tapped his shoulder. "Time is money, pal. Speak your piece or hold your peace."

Knowing he wouldn't be Davis's pal after he stood up to speak, Cash shrugged off the shoulder tap. "Five more minutes and I will," he advised Cleve.

"Mr. Bowman," the mayor said a few moments later from the council table, "we can't wait here all night to hear you out. Frankly, I'm beginning to wonder why we agreed to this impromptu meeting without knowing in advance your reason for requesting it. So far we've gone on faith that you've gathered us all here because you have something vitally important to say. May we know now what it is?"

Cash ran a finger under his collar and straightened his necktie. He looked around for any sign of Larinda. He saw only the expectant faces of his fellow citizens looking back at him. Drawing in a deep breath, he rose from his seat.

"Mr. Mayor, I apologize for the delay and thank everyone here for their patience. I was hoping Ms. Outlaw would be present tonight."

"Since she isn't, let us proceed without her presence, Mr. Bowman."

"Yeah," Cleve muttered. "Let us, please."

Cash had never expected that Larinda wouldn't show. He had never thought he'd have to stand and speak without her there to witness it. His expectation had been to see her face blossom with trust and deepening love when she heard what he had to say. He loved her. She was the primary reason he'd called this meeting. He wanted to be her hero.

He looked down at Dan, the second reason he was here. He wanted to be a hero to his son, too. Few fathers ever got an opportunity like this to do the right thing.

"Mr. Mayor," he began, "members of the council, my fellow Westonians, you all know I've been a strong supporter of Davis Development's subdivision plans. You know I spoke against the operation of a drive-in theater in my neck of the woods at the last meeting."

Larinda heard Cash say "meeting" as she cracked open a rear door of the hall and peered inside. Breathless from rushing, she slipped into the nearest seat in an empty row. No one noticed. Their attention was on the tall, dark, handsome man addressing the council.

Larinda's eyes were also riveted on him from that moment forward. His back was to her and the audience as he faced the council. His shoulders were broad and strong. She loved him.

"I spoke against Larinda Outlaw's operation of that theater," Cash continued, "for two reasons. I intended to buy one of Cleve Davis's houses, for one thing. For another, I didn't want the major hassle that movies would have caused me at the flea market. Since taking that stand, however, I've stumbled on something that reverses the position I took then."

The room buzzed. Larinda blinked. She saw Cleve Davis stand up behind Cash.

"What the hell?" Cleve exclaimed.

The mayor rapped his gavel. "Mr. Davis, please sit down and wait your turn to speak." He paused for Davis to grudgingly obey, then instructed, "Continue, Mr. Bowman. What have you stumbled on?"

"Foxes," Cash said.

"Foxes?" the mayor echoed. "Foxes?" repeated everyone else in the hall, Larinda, as well.

Cash nodded. "Foxes live in the fields surrounding the Moonglow. And not just any old foxes. What we have out there is a mated pair of San Joaquin kit foxes and two nursing cubs, maybe more. They're an endangered species."

He turned to Dan who handed him several news clippings stapled together. "These," Cash went on, "are articles and photos we've all read and seen in *The Westonian* over the past year. They're related to endangered wildlife here in the Central Valley."

Cleve rushed to his feet again. "Are you crazy, Bowman?" Reaching around Cash, he ripped the articles from his hand. "Didn't that owl thing up north teach you to keep your trap shut about garbage like this?"

Cash kept his clenched fist at his side, but only because of Dan. "Chill it, Cleve," he ordered dark and low, "I've felled bigger trees than you before breakfast."

"Mr. Davis!" the mayor rebuked, rapping his gavel again. "Restrain yourself, please. Go on, Cash."

Cash held up a book. "This is *California's Wild Heritage*," he said. "It's subtitled *Threatened and Endangered Animals in the Golden State*. My son, who discovered the foxes first, brought this book home. He'd like to tell you what's endangered here in the Central Valley. Dan?"

Dan stood. He blushed and grinned up at his father before ticking off on his hand, "Antelope squirrels, kangaroo rats, Aleutian Canada geese . . ." He faltered for a moment, counting to himself, then continued, "Winter-run Chinook salmon on the Sacramento River, *and*—" he held up his thumb "—San Joaquin kit foxes. That's not all, but it's enough."

Astonished and bursting with love and pride, Larinda broke into applause. Startled, the council looked over to where she sat. Cash, Dan and everyone else craned around. Seeing Larinda, Eva Maycomb took up her applause. Like a wave, it spread through the hall.

"Well," said the mayor to Larinda when it died down, "it's about time you got here."

"I promised I would," Larinda said, putting her heart into a smile directed at Cash and Dan.

Daunted by the applause, Dan squirmed back into his seat and hid his red face. Cash put his deepest feelings into an eloquent gaze at Larinda.

"Damn you, Cash," Cleve sputtered. "I—"

A sharp rap of the mayor's gavel cut him off. "Don't provoke me, Mr. Davis," the mayor acidly advised. To Cash, he said, "Continue."

Turning away from Cleve's upraised fist with great effort, Cash referred again to the wildlife book. "According to this," he said, "more than one hundred species of birds, mammals, reptiles, amphibians, insects, mollusks, fish and crustaceans—" he paused for breath "—are disappearing in this state."

He opened the book to the heart-tugging fox photo and held it up for all to see, adding, "That's what we'll never have again if housing takes over the fields around the Moonglow."

"You've seen these foxes?" asked one of the towncouncil members.

"I have, twice now. Dan has also taken snapshots of them. I took his snaps to a biology professor at the university here, and she confirmed the species for us."

Thinking fast despite the rush of emotion misting her eyes, Larinda shot to her feet. "Mr. Mayor, may I please say a few words at this point, since I own property where the foxes live?"

The mayor raised his eyebrows in question at Cash, who nodded. "Fine by me," Cash said, a small smile on his lips at her quick show of support. He pivoted around to look at her, his smile widening.

"It seems clear to me," she began, "that the Moonglow has been coexisting in harmony with the wildlife in the fields all along. I suspect it presents no threat to these *rare* animals." She saw Cash wink approvingly at her emphasis on that adjective. "A subdivision, however, would spell doom for them."

Larinda surveyed the sea of faces turned to her. "Outdoor drive-ins are an endangered species, too," she added. "I confess that when I first came up with my plan to bring the Moonglow back, I had selling it later in mind. Now I can truthfully say I'll change my mind if the council decides to reexamine the issue—and the subdivision zoning in that area."

"Mr. Mayor," Cleve thundered. "This is—"

"Shut up, Cleve," barked the mayor. "You lost your turn a long time ago. Mrs. Maycomb has her hand up, over there. Eva, what did you want to say?"

"It's Weston's civic responsibility to preserve its fox habitat *and* its outdoor drive-in," Eva declared. "What is the Central Valley without its unique and precious wildlife?"

"Hear, hear," Mrs. Soames piped up.

"What is a California community without a drive-in?" Eva further inquired. She looked at Cash and smiled. "And what is a drive-in without a clean, old-fashioned flea market these days?"

All around, a babble of agreement and protest rose. The mayor hammered his gavel to no avail. Cash looked back across the rows of seats and bobbing heads to where Jeffie Potts sat with his parents. Jeffie waved, at which Cash took Dan's hand and started toward Larinda.

"Wow, Dad," Dan enthused, "you were super-duper."

"So were you," Cash assured, leading him to Larinda.

After Dan gave her a big hug of greeting, Cash took her in his arms and kissed her right there in front of everyone. Watching them, Dan clapped in glee.

"I'm staying at Jeffie's tonight," Dan told Larinda when Cash ended the kiss. "See ya later," he said, hugging them both again before skipping off to join the Potts family.

Cash and Larinda were heading out the door for a more private kiss, when Cleve Davis's hammy hand closed over Cash's shoulder and hauled him back a step.

Lips drawn back in a grimace, Cleve snarled, "You dirty son of a—"

Just as Cleve raised his arm to strike, Cash's fist shot out. Davis fell flat on his back.

Cash left his silent opponent and led Larinda away.

"My hero," Larinda exulted on the short walk to Cash's Chevy. She curled her hand into his and brought his reddened knuckles to her lips. "All mine," she murmured.

"Am I, Red? Your hero? The guy you can trust?"

"Yes. I misjudged you so much before now."

"Not so much," he said, shaking his head. "I didn't put my best foot forward until tonight."

"Neither did I, the way I was always putting money before love. After this, how could I *not* trust you?" Nearing his car, she saw that it was polished to a high shine. The chrome gleamed and the top was down.

He opened the door for her to get in. Vaulting over the door on his side, he slid behind the steering wheel. "Where to?"

"The Moonglow will do. If you give Walt the rest of the night off."

"I already did."

Larinda got as close to Cash as she could on the front seat. "Let's go, then," she purred, draping her leg over his and stroking her fingers up the inside of his thigh.

He growled in reply, "What do you have in mind?"

"Red on red after a reunion in the back seat. Also, everything else you promised before I left."

"*Everything?*"

"To the very—," she traced the leg seam of his pants inward "—last—" she cupped her palm to the cross of his mid-seam "—detail."

The Chevy's tires squealed as Cash took off.

In the time it took them to race out of town to their own personal passion pit, Larinda got out of most of her clothes and got Cash out of half of his. His tie went flying from her fingers into the warm spring night. Her panty hose met the same airy fate.

At the Moonglow, Cash pulled the Chevy to a halt in front of the big screen. A full moon hung in the star-spangled sky above it. He turned to Larinda.

"All night long," he promised.

Giddy and giggling, stripped down to scanty panties and a lacy bra, Larinda pushed him into the back seat and went tumbling after him.

Cash settled over her, his zipper open where he swelled hard and ready. "So, Red," he whispered. "You're not one for the money now?"

"Not if we're two for the show—and the flea market, Cash."

"We could still get voted down at city hall after the dust settles," he cautioned.

Larinda gazed over his shoulder at the stars above. "Not according to Mrs. Soames and the spiritual ozone.

She *knows*, you know. She hasn't been wrong yet. And if Chester and Jethro have anything to say about it up there, we're both going to be in business when the dust settles. We'll want exactly what we have."

"You're sure you want what we have right now?"

She nodded. "Yes, thanks to Jethro's will and Chester's philosophy, I do."

"Me, too. We owe them a debt for bringing us together."

"We'll pay them both back," she assured, "with outdoor movies and a thriving flea market and a brother and sister for Dan."

"Mmmm. When do we start practicing for that last part, Red?"

"Now," Larinda whispered, lifting her lips to his. "Right now."

This month's
irresistible novels from

Temptation

NAUGHTY TALK by Tiffany White
Live the fantasy...in Lovers and Legends

*Once upon a time a handsome knight errant went searching for
the secrets of women's deepest desires*—or so the story goes.
Nicole Hart wanted revenge on Anthony Gawain.
Masquerading as a provocative sex therapist on his TV show
presented just the opportunity Nicole needed to teach him a
thing or two...

JUST THE WAY YOU ARE by Elise Title

Why had she married uptight Mike Powell? But the minute
Lucy had signed the divorce decree she was sorry. Mike had
had it with his wife's fiery temper. But now they were parting
he remembered just how vivacious and sultry she could be.
What lengths would they go to to get back together again?

DECEPTIONS by Janice Kaiser

As a teenager, Darcy Hunter was guiltily infatuated with her
older sister's fiancé, Kyle Weston. Following her sister's tragic
death, Kyle dropped out of Darcy's life—but not fully out of
her heart and fantasies. What would she do now that she was
being drawn back into his dangerous circuit?

SEEING RED by Roseanne Williams

When Larinda Outlaw inherited a run-down business, she
thought her dreams had come true. Now she could get hold of
some cold, hard cash. Instead she got hot, sexy Cash Bowman
who stood in the way of her plans to sell.

Spoil yourself next month
with these four novels from

Temptation

THE OTHER WOMAN by Candace Schuler
This is the first in a blockbusting **Hollywood Dynasty** trilogy.

The newspapers were full of gossip about Tara
Channing—TV's sexiest seductress and star of the new movie
The Promise—and her surprising relationship with Gage
Kingston whose family was a legend in Hollywood. He had
sworn never to fall for another actress, and Tara had had her
own share of heartache, too. Would their love survive all the
media attention?

YOU GO TO MY HEAD by Bobby Hutchinson
With her company on the verge of bankruptcy, the only person
who could save Annabelle Murdoch's dream was Ben Baxter.
But, sexy, laid-back Ben wasn't interested in business. He was
interested only in awakening her to the pleasure of life and
love…

LOVESTORM by JoAnn Ross
Saxon Carstairs was a loner, but his isolation was shattered
when gorgeous Madeline washed up half-dead on his beach.
Helpless and unable to remember anything beyond her name,
Madeline aroused all Sax's instincts—protective, heroic *and*
carnal.

THE MISSING HEIR by Leandra Logan
Responsible for locating Douglas Ramsey's missing heir,
Caron Carlisle was shocked when the person who said he
could solve the mystery turned out to be Rick Wyatt—the man
who had broken Caron's heart years before.

$\boxed{4}$ *Temptations and* $\boxed{2}$ *FREE gifts for you*

Here's an invitation for you to treat yourself for FREE to all that's most daring and provocative in modern love stories, with 4 Temptation romances, a CUDDLY TEDDY and a special MYSTERY GIFT. And, if you choose, go on to enjoy 4 exciting Temptations each month, delivered direct to your door for just £1.95 each. Complete the coupon below and post it to: **Reader Service, FREEPOST, PO Box 236, Croydon, Surrey CR9 9EL.**

- - - - - - `NO STAMP REQUIRED` - - - - - -

Yes! Please rush me 4 FREE Tempations and 2 FREE gifts! Please also reserve me a Reader Service subscription. If I decide to subscribe I can look forward to receiving 4 Temptations for just £7.80 each month, delivered direct to my door, postage and packing FREE. If I choose not to subscribe I shall write to you within 10 days - and still keep the free books and gifts. I may cancel or suspend my subscription at any time. I am over 18 years of age.

Ms/Mrs/Miss/Mr _____ EP72

Address _____

_____

Postcode _____ Signature _____

mps
MAILING
PREFERENCE
SERVICE